# The Secret of
# the Strawbridge Place

Kate would never have spent so much time pursuing the Secret if she hadn't broken her arm. And she would never have broken her arm if she hadn't been afraid of hobos. So the whole adventure was her brother Josh's fault. He was the one who had taken her down, that first day of summer, to spy on the hobo camp by the railroad trestle. It was because the hobos had seen them that they both ran and Kate fell.

There was nothing to do after that. What can you do in the summer with your arm in a cast? "Search for the Secret," said her mother. Rumor had it that somewhere in or around their house was a secret room that had been used as a station on the Underground Railroad before the Civil War.

Kate's search for the room was halfhearted until she met Oscar, who in an accident also precipitated by Josh, broke his ankle. As Cripples Incorporated they began a systematic search that led to a cave, some mysterious boxes, and finally, to near disaster for Kate.

Kate and Josh and Oscar, and his sister, Simone, lived in the early 1930s, and whatever happened that was fun, they had to make happen themselves.

# The Secret of the
## Strawbridge Place

*The Secret of the*

by HELEN PIERCE JACOB

ILLUSTRATED BY A. DELANEY

# Strawbridge Place

Atheneum · New York · 1976

Library of Congress Cataloging in Publication Data

Jacob, Helen Pierce.
The secret of the Strawbridge Place.
SUMMARY:   Two friends search for the secret of an
old house rumored to have been a station on the
Underground Railroad. Then one of them disappears.
[1. Mystery and detective stories]   I. Delaney,
A.   II. Title.
PZ7.J139Se        [Fic]        75–23199
ISBN 0–689–30504–4

Published simultaneously in Canada by
McClelland & Stewart, Ltd.
Manufactured in the United States of America
H. Wolff, New York
Book design by Mary M. Ahern
First Edition

FOR MOTHER AND DAD

# The Secret of the
# Strawbridge Place

# *Chapter 1*

"Blackie," Kate said to the pregnant cat stretched out in her lap. "It's the very first day of summer vacation. No school for three whole glorious months, Blackie, imagine. You know what I'm going to do this summer, Blackie?" She felt the cat's soft ears. "I'm going to practice the sidestroke until I can swim with Dad out to the breakwater when we go to the lake. I hope the whole summer is hot, hot, like it is today. Then Dad'll take us to the lake every single night. Wouldn't that be swell, Blackie?" But the big cat purred indifferently at all this talk about water and dropped her head onto Kate's bare leg.

The screen door burst open. Josh flopped down on the top step above her and stretched out his stinking rotten sneakers near her face. "It's four hours until the Witherspoon's train comes," he said. "You aren't going to sit here all morning watching for them, are you?"

3

"Move." Kate ignored his question and pinched her nose closed. "I was here first." He moved his feet an inch.

"You won't see anything. They'll be inside the limousine." He shifted restlessly. "Let's me and you do something."

Kate let go of her nose and looked back at him in surprise. He never wanted to do things with her. But today their brother Nathan had, for the first time, gone with Dad to the garage to be apprenticed. Josh leaped to the grass, turned a somersault and stood on his head, waving his offending sneakers in the air. "What'll we do?" he shouted in an upside-down voice.

She was flattered by his unexpected attention, yet all she really wanted to do was stay on the cool stone step, pet Blackie, and watch for the limousine that would come down the hill, meet the train, and return carrying Old Mr. Porch's daughter and two grand-children back to the stone mansion on top. Old Mr. Porch had lived there forever, but his daughter, Elizabeth, hadn't. Years ago she had gone to New York, married an Englishman, and this was her first visit home. The whole town had been gossiping about her visit for weeks, and Kate didn't want to miss her arrival.

Josh did cartwheels down the front walk and landed easily on his feet. "Don't sit there like a zombie. Think of something to do. It's the first day of vacation," he yelled throwing his arms wide into the summer freedom. Just then a faint train whistle echoed through the warm fragrant air. "Got it!" he said moving very close so that no one would hear. "Let's go spy on the hobo camp."

Kate's skin goose bumped, and she shook her head emphatically.

"Fraidy cat," Josh taunted. "Fraidy cat, fraidy cat."

"I'm not," Kate said. "You know it's forbidden."

"Nathan and I've been there lots of times, and Dad's never found out." Kate wasn't surprised. Once Dad forbade something, Josh was sure to do it. "Lots and lots of times," Josh repeated. "But not today, I guess. My sissy sister's too scared."

"I'm not a sissy!"

"I *dare* you."

Stung, Kate sprang up, scattering Blackie from her lap. They raced around the huge old house, past the low, oddly shaped garage-shed, the big red barn and over the pasture gate. The cows looked up lazily as they ran past and disappeared over the riverbank. They climbed down the steps cut into the steep bank and started up the trail. Underbrush covered the valley, and Kate and Josh moved Indian file down the path along the Grand River.

Kate lagged. Her armpits were wet with nervousness. She wished Josh hadn't dared her. She stopped to tie her shoe. She retied it twice. Josh hopped from foot to foot. "Quit stalling," he said.

"I'm not stalling, I'm tying my shoe," Kate said indignantly. Why had she come? She was afraid of hobos . . . ragged men with eyes too big for their faces; always at the back door asking for food.

The train whistle sounded nearer this time, and Josh looked up through the trees at the bridge high above them. The freight rolled onto the trestle puffing smoke into the clear morning air. "Hurry up," Josh urged. "With all this racket, the hobos won't hear us coming." He ran down the trail and veered off into the underbrush. Kate hurried after him, hating herself.

The freight roared across the trestle as Josh pushed his way toward the abandoned cabin where the hobos had made their camp. They were close now. Josh dropped to his knees and crept forward like a cat stalking a bird. Kate crawled reluctantly after him. He moved some tall weeds an inch or two. The spy hole revealed the clearing and the ramshackle cabin. Kate forced herself to look. A shapeless figure sat before the cabin watching a chicken on a stick over a small fire. Josh looked over at her and grinned wickedly.

Several minutes passed, then Kate's stomach cramped. Someone was coming down the steep trail from the railroad. She sucked in her breath. Two hobos stepped into the clearing, one waving a narrow brown bottle.

"Tolt you I smelt somethin'," slurred the one with the bottle. He took a lurching step toward the fire and reached for the chicken. The huddled hobo rose cursing.

"That there's my bird, and you keep your filthy paws off it, hear." He was bent like a string bean, and his pants were tied about his caved-in stomach with a piece of rope. The two younger hobos crouched and began to circle slowly toward him.

Two against one. Kate ducked her head, but Josh's eyes glittered.

The older hobo put out a placating hand. "Now, fellers, there's a wing there for all of us." But the two younger men were too drunk to be placated. They both leaped at once, and the three went down. The chicken hobo shook free and got to his knees, but the others were on him again. He tried to dodge, but they knocked him backwards into the fire, upsetting the chicken. His shirt smoldered. Kate bit her knuckle and almost screamed. Josh inched forward, his mouth open.

The hobo moaned and rolled over and over, smothering the glowing edges of flame. One of the young hobos snatched the half-cooked chicken, dropped it like a hot potato, swore, and then scooped it out of the dirt and staggered off toward the river. The other melted into the weeds just a few feet from Kate and Josh. The beaten hobo lay groaning and writhing in the deserted clearing.

Kate's heart turned sidewise. "Josh, he's hurt. Do something," she pleaded softly.

"Can't do nothing," Josh whispered back. "Let's scram." But Kate couldn't move. Then something she couldn't help made her get up and step into the clearing, her hand outstretched. The hobo roared an oath and rolled toward her. Kate stood paralyzed, then she was almost pulled from her feet. Josh didn't let go of her arm until they were on the path.

"You stupid jerk. What do you think you're doing, going up to that guy? . . ."

"Where did those others go with the chicken?" Kate asked coming out of her trance.

"Down by the river," Josh answered. Kate started to run. "Hold your horses," he called. "They couldn't care less about us. All they wanted was that chicken. Couldn't you tell they were starving? It was the starving that made them fight. Those young punks probably haven't eaten in days. If that chicken hadn't been there, they would have killed the old hobo and roasted him."

"Oh no." Kate crowded up close to him.

"Sure," Josh said nonchalantly. "Starvation makes you inhuman. I've read about shipwrecked people in lifeboats who ate each other."

"That's only in books," Kate said in a quavery voice.

Suddenly Josh stopped, and Kate crashed into him she was so close on his heels. Her skin shrank up tight.

There, a few yards ahead in the middle of the river path, crouched the two young hobos sucking on chicken bones and drinking from the narrow brown bottle.

"Hey," one started unsteadily toward them. "Two little plump ones for dessert."

Josh and Kate leaped aside into the underbrush. They clawed at the bushes, running, falling, struggling to their feet, running, running. Panting they reached the bank and scrambled pell-mell up the steep slope, clutching at roots and rocks, pulling themselves up in desperate haste. They never stopped to listen for their pursuers. They didn't look back. Josh outstripped her and vanished over the top of the bank.

Panic welled through Kate. She didn't dare call after him. She didn't dare look back. She was alone. Alone in the river valley with those two hobos who wanted her for dessert. Wildly she grabbed for a tree root and pulled hard. The rotten root gave way, and she fell back; toward the river, toward the hobos, toward capture.

# Chapter 2

She never knew how long she lay sprawled around the huge tree that had broken her slide, but when she opened her eyes it was quiet. She listened for the hobos, but the only sounds were bird songs and the buzz of insects. Slowly she sat up. Her body ached, but her right arm pained fiercely. It was terribly swollen around the elbow. She grasped the low spreading branch of an evergreen to steady herself. The limb pulled aside, and for a moment she forgot everything. Beside a huge rock was a small dark hole big enough for her to crawl into. She slipped under the limb to look closer.

It looked like the entrance to a cave!

A shout from the hobo camp startled her. Panic-stricken, she scrambled from under the limb and up the bank, steadying herself with her good arm. At last she reached the top. Holding her arm against her side, she crossed the pasture, awkwardly climbed the

gate and went to the house. "Mom!"

The house was silent. She sank down on the porch. "Josh!" she yelled. She didn't care if he called her a sissy a hundred times. Her arm throbbed. She wanted someone . . . anyone. "Josh!" she screamed. He always disappeared when he'd done something wrong.

The summer . . . the sidestroke . . . the Witherspoon kids . . . Josh . . . hobos . . . the limousine . . . the noon train . . . all circled in confusion through her mind. Nausea boiled in her stomach. The Model A Ford turned in the drive just as she threw up.

"There you are," Mom said easing her pregnant abdomen from behind the wooden steering wheel and stepping onto the running board. "I called and called before I left for the market . . . where were you and Josh?" Kate couldn't lift her head. Yellow gunk dribbled from her mouth onto the porch.

"That's vomit," Margaret said pointing with a fat finger.

"Sakes alive, honey." Mom was beside her in an instant. "What's the matter?"

"I'm sick," Kate mumbled. Vomit oozed between her teeth. Margaret crouched down and peered at her.

"It's all right now, Mother's here. Let me . . . oh, Kate . . . your arm." She put cool fingers on the swollen elbow, and Kate moaned. "That looks broken to me. I'd better call Dr. Marsh." She held Kate's head until she finished throwing up, then led her into the little bathroom off the den and wiped her streaked face and cleaned her mouth. Josh appeared from nowhere and quietly unloaded the groceries. He knew he had it coming if Kate talked, but Mom was too busy calling the doctor to ask. They all climbed into the car and drove quickly to the hospital.

It was broken in two places. Kate gritted her teeth as Dr. Marsh and his nurse, Miss Pea, put on a heavy plaster cast from wrist to shoulder and tied a sling around her neck. Kate moved her fingers tentatively but even that hurt. "Relax, don't fight the cast, and above all, keep it *dry*," Miss Pea warned severely.

"Six weeks," Doc said. He patted her absently on the head as if she were three instead of eleven and three-quarters. Kate felt like a convict hearing his prison sentence. No sidestroke practice . . . no swimming to the breakwater with Dad . . . the summer ruined before it even got started. . . .

Mom draped Kate's blouse around her shoulders, and they climbed back into the Model A. It was hot. As they turned into the drive, Mom almost side-swiped the birch tree as she pointed up at the turreted mansion on the hill. "Almost noon," she said. "Train's due."

Margaret and Josh raced each other to the edge of

the road. Kate followed slowly, hugging her blouse about her, and stood half-hidden behind the maple tree. The sling cut into her neck. She wiggled her fingers again and winced at the pain.

"There it is," Margaret cried jumping up and down and pointing. The great gray limousine came slowly down the hill, the chauffeur stiff in his gray visored cap and leather driving gauntlets. Margaret waved. The chauffeur stared straight ahead. The great gray car proceeded majestically around the curve of Bank Street to the railroad station. The noon train whistled faintly, then in a few minutes rumbled across the trestle, whistled again and slowed to a stop, hissing and puffing. Soon the great gray car returned, suitcases piled high on the luggage rack on the roof. The curtains were pushed back, and the windows rolled down. A girl with long blond hair held back with a wide hairband looked out eagerly as the car slid silently by. Josh and Margaret waved, and the girl waved back.

The next thing Kate knew, Mom was calling her. She dragged into the kitchen. Mom held out an old blue shirt of Nathan's. "I cut the sleeve out." Kate shrugged off her blouse, put her cast through the hole, then Mom buttoned the shirt and retied Kate's sling. "Never did ask you how it happened," Mom said gently.

"Josh and I were on the riverbank, and I slipped

on some moldy leaves." Mom nodded. Things just happened to Kate.

"Time for lunch," she called from the front screen.

"That girl has hair just like mine," Margaret said sweeping her gold-brown curls into her soup. "I hope she likes *Peter Rabbit* and paper dolls and jacks . . ."

"She's more Josh's age, I believe." Mom sat down, her hand on her abdomen. "And the boy's older."

Kate spilled her tomato soup all over the freshly ironed tablecloth.

"Dopey," Josh jeered.

"What an unkind thing to say," Mom said frowning at him. "She couldn't help it. We all know that things just happen to Kate."

Kate glared at Josh. This hadn't just happened. She opened her mouth to tell, then clamped it shut again. The hobo camp was forbidden to all of them, not just Nathan and Josh, and if she tattled, Dad would find out and then . . . oh boy!

As soon as she could, she excused herself, captured Blackie and walked swiftly away from the house. She had to be by herself. She looked up fleetingly at the round towers of the mansion. Did rich people eat tomato soup? Or did they have lunches of tiny white crustless sandwiches and chicken salad cradled in fresh tomato wedges garnished with chilled watercress? Someday she'd look up watercress in the dictionary and find out just what it was.

She hurried by the big vegetable garden, choked with weeds, and ducked into the forest of pines that stretched up the hill, avoiding the corner of the woods where the graves of the Strawbridge family were. She found her secret place, sat down cross-legged and settled Blackie in her lap. Her arm hurt so much she began to cry. She hated Josh . . . absolutely positively hated him more than any living soul on earth. He'd ruined her whole summer, and he was gloating because she couldn't tell. She stuck out her tongue toward the house. Someday she'd kill him.

The pungent perfume of the pines surrounded her. Gradually the solitude and Blackie's purring lulled her into thoughtfulness. What was she going to do with six whole long weeks with her arm in a cast? Reading was OK, and she loved the library, but summer vacation was for other things besides books. Last year she'd gone to Y camp and . . .

A shout made her sit up. "We're not lost, Simone. Here's a path." Kate listened, and Blackie lifted her head and turned narrowed eyes toward the noise. They sat still as fawns.

Someone crashed about near them, then a boy blundered into her secret place. He stopped short in surprise. "What in the sam hill? . . ." he said backing away. He was skinny, and his horn-rimmed glasses hung halfway down his narrow, pointed nose. His shoes and knickers looked immaculately white and very hot. "Hey, Simone, in here," he called. "I've found something." He said "something" as if he'd just seen a strange animal in the zoo.

Kate bristled. Who'd he think he was anyway? His grandfather might be the richest man in Ashtabula, but so what.

Simone came ducking under the pines toward his voice. Her hairband was gone, and her disheveled hair was tied back with her belt. "What did you do to your arm?" she demanded without preliminaries.

"Broke it," Kate said. She looked from one to the other. Definitely chicken salad and watercress and not tomato soup. She tried to hide her sneakers with the holes over each big toe under her.

"When?"

"Today."

"How?"

"Hobos were chasing me." Simone knelt down before her and pushed her face close.

"Real, honest-to-goodness hobos?" she asked, her eyes glittering just like Josh's. "Like the hobos we saw from the train?"

"Real, honest-to-goodness hobos," Kate repeated, forgetting her aching arm. "Those awful scary men and I wish I hadn't gone, but Josh dared me and they have a camp down under the trestle. One old hobo in pants tied with a rope had a chicken, and two young punks who were starving came along with a bottle, and they fought over it."

"The bottle?" Oscar asked.

"No, the chicken."

"Who won?" Simone asked.

"The two young punks. Josh said they were starving."

"Who's Josh?"

"The biggest creep in the world," Kate yelled. Simone rocked back on her heels. "He's my dumb brother," Kate finished lamely.

"Let's go see the camp." Simone leaped up.

"We can't." Oscar looked lazily at his watch. "Mom said to be home in time for tea, and it's already three-twenty."

Tea? What's that, Kate wondered.

"Yes we *can*." Simone stamped her foot. "Come on . . . you." She stopped and smiled for the first time. "I'm Simone Witherspoon, and this is Oscar. We live in Bermuda, but we go to school in New York, and we're visiting up there." She pointed toward the great pile of gray stone on the hilltop.

Kate almost said, "I know," but didn't. She didn't want them to know she had stood behind the maple tree and watched them go by in their limousine. Blackie, jealous of Kate's inattention, stalked off with her tail in the air.

"I'm Kate Cummings," she said. She got up eagerly. Simone fell into step beside her. Oscar lagged behind. They climbed the pasture fence. The cows, their curiosity aroused by the strange children, ambled toward them. Simone took hold of Kate's good arm and maneuvered her toward them. Kate smiled. The watercress Witherspoons weren't so smart after all. "They're just cows," Kate said grandly. "They won't hurt you once they get used to you."

"But they're awfully big," Simone said nervously. Oscar eyed the cows and sidled to the other side of Simone. Kate laughed. The day suddenly brightened. These city kids were fun.

They reached the edge of the riverbank where the steps started down. "There." Kate pointed.

"You go down *there?*" Simone looked down the steep bank in disbelief.

"Sure, every day," Kate said feeling more superior all the time.

"Maybe we could go tomorrow." Oscar pushed his glasses up his nose and peered nearsightedly into the wild valley.

"Oh, you . . ." Simone whirled on him. "Sissy."

Kate winced. "Tomorrow," Oscar said sensibly. "Come on, sis." He pointed to his watch again. "It's almost three-thirty and Mom said . . ."

"Phooey on Mom, and phooey on you," Simone shouted and ran across the pasture toward the barn.

"Watch out for the patches of cow manure," Kate called. She and Oscar started after her.

"Who's that?" Simone stopped and pointed.

Mr. Elmer was tossing forkfuls of manure from the barn door.

"That's Mr. Elmer," Kate said catching up with her. "He works the farm on shares with Dad." Oscar joined them, head down, watching where he put his white shoes.

"What's that bump on his cheek?" Simone asked. Kate laughed outright.

"That's his tobacco wad." At that minute Mr. Elmer spit, scattering the flies on the manure.

"Stinks." Oscar held his nose and stepped back, his guard down. His white shoe went deep into a round slippery circle of cow dung. His mouth fell open, then he began swearing. Kate was so shocked she didn't laugh. He leaped about like a grasshopper dragging his shoe in the grass, trying to clean the clinging, smelly dung from it. Simone doubled over with laughter.

"I warned you . . ." Kate began helplessly. Oscar continued swearing, using words Kate didn't know existed.

"Come on, clubfoot," Simone said between gasps. "Teatime. Mom'll be delighted with your stinking shoe under the tea table." She raced to the gate and climbed up and over. Oscar followed slowly still twisting and turning his shoe in the grass. Suddenly

Simone stopped. "We'll be over tomorrow," she called.

Kate waved. She hadn't invited them, yet she did a little hop of excitement. The Witherspoon-watercress kids. They hadn't been here two hours and already they were her friends.

She skirted the manure pile. "Hi, Mr. Elmer. See what happened to me today?" She held out her sling. He smiled all the way to his ears. She told him about the accident, but not the part about the hobos, then about meeting the Witherspoon kids. Mr. Elmer spit. The shadow of the barn stretched far across the pasture. "Bye, Mr. Elmer," Kate said. "Got to go." She went across the lawn toward the house.

# Chapter 3

Mom was handing out sandwiches to two hobos on the kitchen porch. Kate ducked into the garage and waited while the ragged men cut across the lawn and went out the drive beyond the lilac bushes. Once she saw them turn into the road, she left her hiding place and raced to the hooked kitchen screen door and rattled it fiercely. Mom let her in. She flung herself into the old chair below the window and kicked her legs noisily against the rungs. Mom returned to the stove where she was stirring flour and lard together for dried beef gravy. "How's the arm?" she asked in a tired voice.

"Hurts." Kate waggled her sling.

"That'll go away soon the doctor said." Mom wiped the sweat from her forehead with her arm.

"I know," Kate said. "But my summer's spoiled. What can you do with a broken arm?"

"Become ambidextrous," Mom said wearily.

"What's that?"

"Using both hands with equal ease." Kate remembered the spilled soup. "Or you could look for the Secret."

"Was this house really on the Underground Railroad?" Kate asked, even though she knew the legend by heart.

"So the story goes." Mom slopped gravy over the side of the skillet, and a raw burned smell filled the kitchen.

"Do you think there's a secret passage?"

"Probably. The Strawbridges were Quakers, and we know that Quakers hated slavery. And Grand River, right out there where you broke your arm, flows into Lake Erie along those docks where the lake boats left for Canada. So it all fits."

"But we've looked and never found anything," Kate complained.

"But you've never looked very hard or very long," Mom reminded her.

She was right, of course. Kate had always suggested the searches, but Nathan had always organized them because he was the oldest. Last Christmas vacation they had done their most serious searching. Nathan had called them all together and had reviewed the evidence.

"The Secret involves the hiding place where the escaping slaves were concealed," he had said deliberately. "That hiding place could be anywhere in the four buildings on the farm: the house, the garage-shed, the barn or the corncrib. But the house is most likely, so we'll start here. I'm going to assign each of you a special section. Josh, you have the second floor. I'll take the cellar and the attic. Kate and Margaret, the first floor. Feel the walls, the woodwork, tap for hollowness, examine the floors . . ."

"Are we looking for slaves?" Margaret had asked. Josh and Kate had laughed, but Nathan hadn't. When you're only five you ask dumb questions.

"No," he'd said. "You'll be looking for a moving panel, a false wall, a trapdoor, any concealed or secret place . . . and the spring, button, rod, knob projection that opens it. It has to be here, the legend says so."

They had gone eagerly to their sections and begun to search. But in ten minutes Margaret went to play with her Christmas presents and didn't come back. Josh said he had to see Mr. Elmer about a cow, but Kate suspected he was jumping in the haymow. Mom had called Kate to help with supper, and only Nathan had worked on, doggedly patting, pressing, hand over hand, searching for the secret spring.

He had called daily meetings so they could report their progress, but there was never anything to report. Finally Mom had made them stop after discovering dirty finger marks all over the bedroom wall.

The screen door rattled, and Dad hollered, "Hey, lady, we ain't bums." Mom brightened, rushed to the screen and unhooked it. "Hot as Hades," Dad said, catching Mom up and giving her a smacking kiss. "Let's go to the lake to cool off."

"Oh yes, let's." Kate jumped up then sank back, her cast suddenly big as the barn. Dad spread his legs and looked down at her.

"Mom called and told me all about your accident," he said. "How is it?"

"OK."

"Hurt?"

"Some."

"Things do happen to you, Kate, don't they?" Dad shook his head. Then he bolted up the back stairs. Nathan gave Kate an understanding wink and followed slowly.

Mom broke into the old hymn "Brighten the Corner Where You Are" as she shoved the skillet filled with the half-done gravy into the refrigerator. She loved the lake. Kate stood by the table feeling very left out as Mom made peanut butter and jelly sandwiches. She scraped carrots and cut celery and wrapped them in waxed paper. "Josh, Margaret, lake, picnic!" she called through the screen. They came in whooping and shoving and raced up the back stairs to change into their suits.

"I don't want to go," Kate said.

"Now, honey, don't spoil it for the rest of us." Mom stuck a hat pin through her floppy straw hat with the broken brim. "You can wade."

Dad drove to the lake, Mom in the back seat between Josh and Nathan so they wouldn't wrestle. The boys rushed across the sand toward their favorite log, hastily spread the blankets, then dashed and dived headlong into the water. Everyone followed them into the wonderfully cool water . . . everyone except Kate. She sat unhappily against the log watching the others. The boys played catch with an old tennis ball. Dad started his ten laps to and from the breakwater, and Mom sat on the sandy bottom, just her head and hat and book above the water. Margaret put her favorite paper doll in the sand and began building a castle for her.

Sweat oozed from Kate's temples and armpits, and she scratched irritably. If it hadn't been for Josh, she'd be out there practicing the sidestroke. . . . Angrily she got up, kicked off her sneakers and digging her heels into the sand, stalked toward the lake's edge.

"You clumsy ox." Margaret rushed at her. "You walked on my dolly." Margaret picked up her dismembered paper doll from a deep heel print. "You've killed her," Margaret shouted, throwing the paper fragments at Kate. Crying, she grabbed up sand in her fists and hurled it at Kate. Kate shook free of her sling and started splattering water at Margaret.

"Girls, girls, Kate, your cast. . . ." Mom warned. Kate straightened up and looked down at her arm. Margaret ran screaming to Mom. "Didn't you hear Miss Pea say . . . above all, keep it dry?" Mom asked, putting her arm around the sobbing Margaret. "Just look at that mess." She picked up a towel and wrapped it around the soggy cast. "Now for goodness sakes, behave yourself."

"She started it," stormed Kate.

"But, honey, you're older. You should know better," Mom said. "Now sit down and be quiet and let me have a moment's peace." She closed her eyes as she said it.

Kate slammed down on the blanket and stuck her legs out defiantly. Mom shook her head in a tired way and returned to her watery seat.

The sun dropped into Lake Erie, and everyone came out and stood about hugging towels. Dad ripped open the brown bag, and Nathan and Josh grabbed for the sandwiches but ignored the celery and carrots. They ate so greedily that Kate remembered the starving hobos with a shudder. Finally they all flopped over to watch for the first star. They sang hymns, but Kate lay silent. The stars appeared one by one. "Which one is the North Star?" she asked Dad. He pointed it out. That was the star that the slaves had followed to freedom. Kate thought idly about the Secret. That might be something she could do with a broken arm . . .

Then Dad got up and stretched. "Workday to-morrow, right Nathan, my boy?" Nathan grunted and dashed for one last plunge. Josh followed. Dad stood with his hands on his hips and smiled, then reached down and began to shake the blankets. "Sure wish we could afford a cottage on the lake for a week this summer," he said.

"I'll never forget that vacation we had three years ago in the Cleverton cottage," Mom said. She sat down on the log and put her arm around Kate. "How's that old arm?"

"OK," Kate said. Mom squeezed her shoulder. The caress eased Kate's feelings, but she didn't let on to Mom. They wended their way across the deserted beach to the car, climbed in, and drove home over quiet country roads.

# Chapter 4

The next morning Blackie swished her tail under Kate's nose, and she woke up sneezing. The heavy cat sat on the sheet smiling at Kate with her yellow eyes. "You're my only friend," Kate whispered reaching out and touching Blackie's delicate belly fur. Outside the window the birch tree drooped motionless in the hot morning.

She rose and washed with left-handed awkwardness. Blackie sat with her tail curled around her as Kate dressed in faded shorts and Nathan's old shirt. They went down the hall together, Kate's shoelaces dangling.

Dad and Nathan were at the table, and Mom was frying mush as Kate and Blackie came in. "How's your arm?" Mom said. Kate put her feet up, and Dad tied her shoes.

"Shouldn't have gotten that cast wet last night, honey." Dad tousled her hair roughly. "Broken arms cost aplenty without extra trips to the doc like this one this morning."

"I couldn't help it." Kate hung her head.

"Things just happen to you, don't they?" Dad lifted her chin. Kate twisted away and slid into her chair, and Blackie leaped into her lap. "But you gotta be more careful." He shook his finger at her. "Money don't grow on trees, Kate, especially not *now*." He took a gulp of hot coffee and looked up at Mom. "Told you about the Morgans, didn't I?"

"No, you didn't," Mom said anxiously.

"Lloyd brought his car into the garage yesterday. Bank finally foreclosed on his farm, and he's leaving for California soon as he can."

"Oh no." Mom's face went all soft.

"Yeah. Said he heard there's work picking fruit out there."

"Picking fruit." Mom shook her head indignantly. "Those two wonderful farmers picking fruit. It just isn't right. When's it going to end, Edgar?"

"Beats me." Dad poured Mom's homemade syrup over his mush. "You'd think times couldn't get worse, then they do. Lloyd didn't pay me a cent. Said he'd send a check from California."

"It's just awful." Mom set a full plate of mush down on the table with a bang. "Isn't there something we can do for them?"

"I did his car for free, didn't I," Dad said. "We gotta live too."

"But we're so lucky, Edgar. The Strawbridge Place is ours, and you haven't lost the garage . . ."

"Yet," Dad said pointedly. "If that President Hoover don't do something mighty quick, we'll be joining Lloyd and Rachel on their trek west. I haven't gotten paid real money for a job all month. I couldn't make Lloyd pay . . . you can't get blood out of a stone . . . but if I don't get some cash soon. . . ." He drank coffee belligerently.

Kate and Nathan looked at each other. When Dad had stopped their allowances last Christmas, they had known something was wrong.

Dad got up, ran his hands over his chest and reached for his shirt with the words "Cummings Bike and Auto Garage" on the back. "Move, son." He nudged Nathan, then grabbed his cap from the peg behind the door. He kissed Mom tenderly. "Take it easy, honey." He squinted at the sun. "It's going to be another scorcher." He and Nathan crossed the yard; Kate and Mom waved to them from the screen door.

"Mom, why couldn't Mr. Morgan pay for his car?"

"Hard times, honey. His farm was mortgaged to the bank, and he couldn't keep up the payments so the bank took it back. He's like a lot of other people who've lost everything . . . homes, farms, stores, jobs. That's why we have so many hobos asking for food. They're men looking for work, any work, wherever they can find it."

"You mean like Mr. Morgan going to California?"

"Like that."

"I'm sorry I got my cast wet," Kate cried. "I didn't know it would cost a lot of money."

"Uh . . . huh," Mom said, but Kate knew she wasn't thinking about casts; she was thinking about Lloyd and Rachel.

After Josh and Margaret had breakfast, they all drove to the hospital, and Kate's cast was repaired. When they got home, Kate went out to the front steps, where Blackie settled in her lap. She hadn't been there five minutes before Mom said from the doorway, "Kate, you have visitors."

Simone and Oscar were a blur through the screen. Kate sprang up excitedly, and the startled Blackie twitched an angry tail as she landed on the porch. "Hi," she said.

"Hi."

"This is my mom," Kate said.

"We introduced ourselves in the kitchen." Mom looked down at them. There was a pause, then Mom took a deep breath. "How's your mother?"

"Fine."

"Does she like being home again?"

"She hasn't said," Oscar said politely. Mom opened her mouth to say more, then sighed and turned away. Simone sat down beside Kate, and Oscar lounged on the porch railing.

"What'll we do?" Simone asked. She sounded just like Josh.

"Want to hear about the Strawbridge Secret?" Kate blurted out.

"A real secret or make-believe?" asked Simone.

"Real," Kate said. Oscar moved a mite closer, his lazy eyes on Kate. "It's the Strawbridge Secret. It's about this house. It was Clayton and Sarah Strawbridge's house, and they hated slavery so much that they made it a station on the Underground Railroad and helped the slaves escape to Canada. There's a secret place where they kept the slaves, but no one has ever found it except we've looked, and it's been a bust, and that's the legend."

"You're not kidding are you?" Oscar said suddenly moving down very close to her.

"She's pulling your leg," Simone laughed. "Whoever heard of a real mystery right next door?" But Kate ignored her and looked straight at Oscar.

"No," she said solemnly. "It's true. It has to be true. Dad says if a legend lasts as long as this one has, then there must be truth behind it."

"How old is it?"

"About eighty years."

"But you said you've looked and it's always been a bust," Simone said,

"That doesn't prove anything," Oscar said. "Obviously they haven't looked in the right place yet."

"What'll we do?" Simone asked again, losing interest in the Secret. She twitched, ready to fly in any direction there was action. Just then Mr. Elmer rattled down the drive behind the lilac bushes in his rickety truck. Simone was after it. Kate and Oscar followed talking earnestly.

They entered the barn and found Simone squatting in the clean straw watching Mr. Elmer milk Bessy. After a minute Josh and Margaret burst in. Kate scowled at the intruders. Oscar and Simone were her friends, she'd seen them first. Josh gave Simone a perfunctory look and turned to Oscar. "Want to jump in the hay?"

"Do *what?*" Oscar asked incredulously.

"Jump in the haymow?" Josh repeated.

"I do." Simone moved toward Josh. "Show me." Josh glanced from Simone to Oscar.

"Come on," he said. Simone and Margaret were on his heels, and Oscar moved indolently after them. He leaned against a post.

"Like this," Josh said, giving Oscar a disgusted look. He ran up the ladder and across the platform, leaped far out and landed in the soft hay with a

swish. Carefully he slid down the smooth side of the mow to the floor and scrambled up the ladder again. "Hey, Kate, shoot me," he called.

If only she had a real gun. Kate lifted her heavy cast and pointed her arms as if holding a gun toward Josh. As Josh leaped from the platform, Kate made a sound like a shot. Josh twisted dramatically in the air, clutched his chest, and fell limply into the hay.

"Hey, watch me." Margaret flew up the ladder. She ran, leaped and landed on her bottom in the hay. Cautiously she slid down to the cement floor and went up the ladder again.

Simone eyed her. Margaret was only five. Suddenly Simone went up the ladder. She ran across the platform, stopped at the edge, then closed her eyes and jumped. Her dress ballooned about her as she fell into the hay a few feet below.

"I did it, I did it!" she shouted bouncing about, tossing hay everywhere. "Come on, Oscar, it's fun." She slid carefully out of the mow just as Margaret and Josh had and raced up the ladder again. "Hey, shoot me, Josh." Simone spurted across the platform. She jumped, Josh shot her, and she clasped her shoulder and fell into the hay. "That's swell," she shrieked, sliding out instantly and racing up the ladder for another turn. "Hey, watch this, everybody." She charged across the platform and dived headfirst into the hay.

"I'm Batman," Josh yelled. He spread his arms and dived near her. Oscar decided he had observed long enough, went gingerly up the ladder, stalked to the edge of the platform, stood estimating the distance to the hay below, held his nose and stepped off, feet first.

"See, fun, huh?" Simone threw hay at him. They cavorted about in a cloud of dust. Josh dived near Oscar, and they started a shoving match. They shouted and wrestled. The hay flew.

"Hey, watch out!" Josh yelled, but it was too late. Oscar slipped over the edge of the mow to the cement floor below. His leg crumpled under him, and his glasses flew off. He lay white and still.

Kate was beside him in an instant. The others slid down the mow and gathered around him. Silence filled the lofty barn, and the dust motes swirled in the beams of sunshine that came through the knot-holes.

Mr. Elmer stepped between Kate and Simone. Without a word he lifted Oscar as easily as if he'd been a kitten and headed for the house. Kate picked up his shattered glasses and followed. Josh ran ahead and banged on the hooked screen door. "Mom," he shouted. She gasped as Mr. Elmer carried Oscar to the couch and put him down.

"Monkeying around in the haymow, slipped, fell, hurt his leg," Mr. Elmer said around his tobacco plug.

"What'll I do?" Mom looked from Oscar's limp form to Mr. Elmer. "Call the doctor or Elizabeth?"

"Call Mom," Simone said decidedly. "I'll call her. Where's the phone?" She followed Mom from the room. "She's coming with Flint," she said a minute later. Mom was putting cold washcloths on Oscar's forehead. He lay stone still.

The limousine turned in the drive and stopped by the side porch. Mrs. Witherspoon flew out. She wore the highest heels Kate had ever seen, and she smelled like a lilac bush. Oscar moaned as she bent over him. Mom stepped back, but she didn't take her eyes off Mrs. Witherspoon.

"How'd this happen?" Mrs. Witherspoon demanded frowning up at Mr. Elmer. Mr. Elmer locked his arms across his chest, clamped his teeth over his wad and stood silent. Mom opened her mouth, but Josh rushed ahead of her.

"We were just fooling around . . ."

"Where?" Mrs. Witherspoon snapped picking hay from Oscar's hair.

"In the barn . . . the haymow. We were just jumping around a little, and suddenly Oscar wasn't there."

"The mow's all slidey on the edge," Margaret

piped up. "He fell down."

Mrs. Witherspoon stared at Mr. Elmer. "Wasn't anyone watching them?" she asked. Mr. Elmer looked at Mom. Mom was about to say something when Oscar moaned again and tried to get up. "Lie still." She swept to the door and signaled the chauffeur. Then she nodded curtly to Mom and Mr. Elmer as Flint carried Oscar to the car. The doors slammed, and the limousine drove around the back and out the other drive behind the lilac bushes.

"City folk," Mr. Elmer said to Mom, then he stalked out. Mom sat down abruptly as if her knees had given way.

"Dear God, make him all right," she said to the ceiling.

Stricken, Kate looked after the limousine. She was still holding Oscar's broken glasses. She turned and went slowly to her secret place. Her shoulders drooped as she sat down. They would never be back now. Mrs. Witherspoon wouldn't let them. And Oscar had asked lots of questions about the Secret. . . .

"Please, God, make him all right," she repeated Mom's prayer. Reverently she laid the glasses in with her books and covered them with pine needles. Suddenly she sat up straight.

Mom had called Mrs. Witherspoon . . . Elizabeth.

# Chapter 5

The days lagged by, each hotter than the last. Mom was canning strawberries. She sat at the sink, stemming, singing "Rock of Ages" and "Onward Christian Soldiers." Josh sat next to her, his feet imprisoned in the rungs of a stool. He stemmed in slow motion, protesting every strawberry. Stemming was usually Kate's job, but her cast excluded her from all wet chores, and Josh was her replacement. Righteous retribution surged through Kate every time she saw him immobilized on that stool.

But she wasn't free. She played with Margaret to keep her out of the stemmers' way. They played hopscotch and parcheesi, and she read *Peter Rabbit* to Margaret over and over. But she had some time to herself, and most of it she spent in her secret place in the pines. She'd read right through all Louisa May Alcott's books, and she'd loved each one, but . . .

summer vacation was for "doing things," not reading all day.

The stemming was over, Josh was loose again, and late one morning nine days after Oscar's accident she was sitting in her secret place in the pines reading *Under the Lilacs* for the sixth time, Blackie in her lap. And all at once Simone came crawling toward her.

"It's been dreadful," Simone announced without any greeting. "Mom forbade us ever coming here again, but she's gone to New York and won't be back until Friday, and I'm not afraid of Maida."

"Who's Maida?"

"Grandpa's sourpuss housekeeper."

"How's Oscar?"

"Getting better. He broke his ankle and had a concussion and lost his glasses, but the concussion's gone already, and he's pretty good on his crutches."

"Can he come over?"

"Maybe. What are you doing?"

"Nothing," Kate said. "Nothing at all." She hid her book behind her.

"Yeah," Simone said. "Boring, isn't it? What's Josh doing?"

"Search me," Kate answered. She was elated to have Simone back.

"Let's go find him," Simone said. Kate's face fell,

but she got up and followed.

Josh was playing horseshoes with a vengeance, making up for lost time. He wasn't eager to show Simone how to play, but she was better than no play-mate at all. After horseshoes Josh showed her how to play mumblety-peg. Kate sat abandoned under the oak tree.

The next morning while Kate waited in her secret place, she half hoped Simone wouldn't come. But when she heard the stirrings of the trees and foot-steps, she was glad. She jumped up as Simone came into the clearing. "Oscar!" she yelled.

"Hi." He balanced expertly on his crutches. Simone threw down the bag she was carrying.

"There. See you later." She rushed off and never even spoke to Kate.

"Where's she going?" Kate asked suddenly feeling shy alone with this strange boy.

"To Josh, where else." He sat down unconcerned and put his crutches precisely together beside him. He reached for the bag and began dragging out books. They were all on the Underground Railroad. "I read all these while I was laid up. Thought they'd help us with the Strawbridge Secret."

"You really believe the legend of the Secret?" Kate asked.

"I sure do," Oscar said. "It's the first mystery I've ever heard of outside a book. And I'm going to solve it." He said it like a vow.

"It's my Secret," Kate warned, forgetting she didn't know him very well.

"Mistress." Oscar bowed mockingly from the waist. "May I assist you in your search?" He looked straight into her eyes. Kate's heart bounced up and down. No boy had ever looked at her like that before. She forgot it was exclusively her Secret.

"Well . . . OK," she said weakly.

"Thank you, mistress." He bowed again. "We're a team now, just us cripples, nobody else, OK? Shake." He held out his hand. Kate put hers out, and they shook hands. "Good. Now Cripples Incorporated to work." He pushed his glasses up his nose and turned back to the books. "Mom's going to buy me more books in New York, but these are all I could get my hands on here in Ashtabula." He opened one. "This one has a great map showing the various routes of the Underground Railroad." He pointed out the black lines. "See, that line ends right here in Ashtabula. So the slaves did come this way. Do you know how old the Strawbridge Place is?"

"1851, I think."

Oscar figured rapidly.

"1851—1931. Exactly eighty years ago. The Railroad was at its height about then. In this book it says that one house had a false room next to the chimney. And another had a bookcase that was really a door.

You took out three books and there was the doorknob. And in this one they hid in a cave. It was Negroes and abolitionists and Quakers who manned the stations . . ."

The look on Kate's face halted him. "Cave? Oh, Oscar, really? I know where there's a cave . . . well, I think it's a cave . . . right here."

He dropped the book. "Where?"

"Down next to the hobo camp. I found it the day I broke my arm."

"What are we waiting for?" He grabbed up his crutches and rose, spilling books about him.

They made their way slowly through the pines, and somehow they got over the pasture fence and to the edge of the riverbank where the steps were. The cows ignored the familiar figures. They started down, but after one step Oscar stopped. He looked down the steep bank. "Blast it!" he exploded throwing his crutches back up the bank and falling to his knees. "Why did I have to break my *ankle*? If I'd broken my arm we could go down there." He sat and slammed his crutches against the ground. "Maybe Josh or Simone could come . . ."

"No." Kate turned on him like a wildcat. "Not *them* . . . nor anyone. You just said *we'd* find it, remember, and we just *shook* on it, and you called us *Cripples Incorporated*, remember? Nobody else, just us, you said. It's our Secret. And we'll solve it all by ourselves. And if you don't want to do it that way, then go on back to Boormooda and forget you ever met me or ever heard about the Strawbridge Secret."

"I didn't mean it." Oscar retreated before her tirade. "Bermuda hasn't got Underground Railroads or Secrets. OK, Cripples Incorporated, nobody else, right?"

"Right," Kate nodded, then doubt clouded her face. She looked from cast to cast. "This funny hole I found isn't like a real cave," she said.

"What do you mean not like a real cave?"

"Well, it was just a little hole . . ."

"How'd you say you found it?" Oscar interrupted.

"I pulled on this big limb, and when it moved I saw this rock and this little dark hole beside it."

"Big enough for us to crawl into?"

"Just big enough."

"Blast it!" Oscar's frustration came flooding out again. "We've got to explore it *now*." He began talking rapidly. "We'll need things. First of all, candles and matches . . ."

"Flashlights are better than candles," Kate said. "I got one to take to Y camp last summer . . ."

"Have to have candles," Oscar waved her explanation aside. "To test the air. If the candle doesn't burn, the air's no good, and we could suffocate."

"We'll take both," Kate said.

The sun reached its zenith, and Kate knew it was

almost lunchtime. They agreed to meet after lunch.

When Kate went into the house, the smell of scorched cloth filled the kitchen. "Set the table, dear," Mom sighed as she heaved the iron onto its metal plate and yanked the cord from the light socket. "How can it stay so *hot?*" She fanned wildly with a cardboard fan from Meyers Funeral Home. Kate watched her uneasily as she made jelly sandwiches. Josh and Margaret rattled the hooked screen on the side porch, and Kate ran to let them in.

"She's nervy for a girl," Josh said to Margaret as they slid into their chairs.

"She can stand on her head better than you can," Margaret said, "and her feet don't stink."

"Aww . . . cut it out about my feet." Josh doubled his fists.

"Margaret, don't tease," Mom said. She changed the subject. "How's Oscar?" She'd called the mansion the afternoon of the accident and had been curtly told that he was in the hospital. She hadn't called again.

"He didn't come." Josh began his third sandwich. "He broke his ankle, Simone said."

"I'm surprised Eliza . . . Mrs. Witherspoon let Simone come after what happened?"

"She's gone." Josh burped unexpectedly. Mom frowned, and he straightened up and began to eat very daintily. Margaret giggled.

"Where?"

"New York till Friday." Mom nodded wisely.

"Can't stay away from New York for long, can you?" she said over their heads to the mansion on the hill.

"Why can't she stay away from New York, and why do you call her Elizabeth?" Kate asked. Just then Margaret upset her milk. Mom cleaned up the mess, and their attention reverted to their food. All but Kate's. She kept watching Mom out of the corner of her eye.

After lunch Kate read *Peter Rabbit* to Margaret while Josh dried the dishes, but at quarter to two Mom let them both go. Kate ran to her secret place in the pines. Precisely at two by his watch, Oscar came down the path. Kate had three of the books open before her.

"Which one tells about the cave?" she asked. Oscar settled himself and shuffled the books.

"This one." He found the page and began to read:

Caves were a natural place for concealment for the escaping slaves. Some caves were just temporary hiding places, but others were of a more permanent nature and were furnished much like a room in a house. One notorious cave on the free side of the Ohio River was a famous first station in the free north. Here a free Negro family furnished a large natural cave with rugs, beds, washstands, towels and linens, trunks of clothes for disguises, food, water and candles. The escaping slaves were met at the river's edge and guided to the cave and often remained there for as long as a week while their pursuers passed them by and searched farther north. After the slaves regained their strength, they were spirited from the cave and moved north through the network of stations until they reached Lake Erie and boarded a lake boat for Canada. The trip across the state sometimes took a month, sometimes less time depending on conditions on the Railroad.

Oscar quit reading. Kate wondered if her hole could be anything as grand and exciting as that cave.

Oscar glared down at the white albatross around his ankle. He got up, put his hand on Kate's shoulder and gingerly tested his weight. "The doctor said not to walk on it yet," he said, "but it doesn't hurt a bit."

"Can you crawl?" Kate asked. Oscar burst out laughing.

"Who can't?" he said. Kate laughed too.

"I guess a broken arm's better than a broken ankle," she said.

"Crawl. . . ." Oscar brightened. "You got a rope in that barn somewhere?"

"Don't know, but we can look," Kate said. Oscar picked up his crutches.

"Let's go," he said.

Mr. Elmer was hoeing in the corn field behind the

garage-shed. They looked in the barn and found a neatly coiled rope hanging on a wooden peg. Taking it, they went through the pasture and sat down just below the edge of the riverbank so no one would see them.

"About where is the cave?" Oscar asked.

"Down there." Kate pointed toward the trestle.

"You know exactly?"

"No," Kate admitted. "But I think I can find it again—except . . ."

"Except what?"

"It's practically on top of the hobo camp . . ."

"You're scared of hobos, aren't you?" Kate nodded. Then she told him everything that had happened the day she'd broken her arm.

"Well," Oscar said. "I can't go down there, so it's you or nobody."

Kate took a deep breath. "OK," she said. She got up and walked slowly to the steps and went down. She didn't need two arms for that. She stopped to listen, then ran down the path along the river and veered into the tall underbrush before she could think. She was hidden, but still she felt uneasy and tried to make as little noise as possible as she went toward the bank. She kept looking up trying to spot Oscar. At last she saw him. His white polo shirt gleamed in the sun. "Here," she called. "I'm down here."

"Is the cave there?" Oscar shouted back.

"Wait a sec." Kate looked for the evergreen and the rock. But all the trees looked alike. She moved up and down the bank pulling aside limbs, looking. Where was it? Nervousness made her movements jerky. She kept stopping to listen. She jumped when Oscar yelled.

"Find it?"

"Not yet." Kate became frantic. The giant criss-cross legs of the trestle loomed up through the trees, and the hobo camp was just below. Kate willed her-self closer and closer, but at last she stopped short, unable to go a step nearer the hobo camp.

"Come up," Oscar called. "I've got a plan."

Kate didn't need a second invitation. She rushed to the path, ran to the steps, and flew up as if a whole tribe of hobos were after her. Panting, she reached Oscar. "Something after you?" he said, laughing.

"No," Kate said feeling sheepish. But Oscar was intent on the search.

"First return the rope. We don't want anyone to have a clue as to what we're up to. I'll meet you in the pines." He set off. Kate coiled the rope, took it to the barn and caught up with him at the fence. She held his crutches as he climbed over. They returned to their secret place.

"Now first things first," Oscar announced settling himself. "We need a code."

"Code?"

"Don't you see. There we were shouting about the cave at the top of our lungs up and down the cliff. Anyone could have heard us. Won't be a secret long if we do that. So we have to have code names for things." He searched his pockets. "What can we write on?"

"We'll spell it out with pine needles." Kate picked up three and made an *A*.

"That's thinking." Oscar smiled at her.

"CAVE." Kate placed the needles carefully.

"Becomes HALL," Oscar said. Kate spelled out HALL behind CAVE. "SEARCH FOR will be TOAD. So TOAD HALL will be SEARCH FOR CAVE." Kate spelled with the pine needles. "ROPE?" he mused.

"ROSE," Kate suggested.

"OK," Oscar agreed.

"RIVERBANK?"

"WATER BUG." Kate giggled.

"Great," Oscar said laughing. "Now we need names. Let's see, who'll I be? Hate Oscar. LORD TOAD." His face lighted up. "And you be LADY TOAD. LORD AND LADY TOAD OF TOAD HALL, ROSES FOR M'LORD AND WATER BUGS FOR M'LADY." They burst out laughing. "Now," Oscar became serious again. "We need to be able to communicate in secret. This is a simple code." He began placing pine needles in a certain way. "But nobody in this little town will have ever heard of it, so it'll do." He explained carefully. Kate nodded, too excited to speak. "So if we need to pass messages, we can write in these numbers instead of letters," he said. He brushed his hands together. "That's settled, but HALL isn't."

"I couldn't find HALL, Oscar. All the trees looked alike."

"OK . . . we'll have to wait until I can walk better, I guess. But we got to begin collecting things. I'll bring candles and matches and string . . ."

"I'll bring my flashlight," Kate said.

"I'll bring food . . ."

"And I'll bring a knife and candles, too," Kate said.

"We'll store everything here." He stopped. His face became gloomy.

"What's the matter?" Kate asked.

"My mom. She'll be back on Friday." They fell silent. Then Oscar looked up and said, "But I'll worry about that on Friday. We have three whole days yet." He shoved a book at her. "Read," he commanded. "The more we both know about the Underground Railroad, the better we'll know what to search for."

Kate opened a book, but the words were meaningless. Could she find HALL again? And before Friday?

# Chapter 6

"Where are you off to so early?" Mom asked pulling down the blind to keep the fierce June sun out of the kitchen. Nathan and Dad weren't down for breakfast yet.

"Oh, no place particularly, just the pines." Kate set her breakfast dishes in the sink. Blackie curled her tail around her bare leg and meowed demandingly.

"Feed Blackie, please, before you vanish. The baby won't let me bend down to get the dish," Mom said her hand on her bulge. Kate spooned food into the clean bowl under the stove. She gave Blackie's back a quick swipe as she ran out. She had more important things to do today than to linger over cats. She dashed to WATER BUG. She was going to find HALL, hobos or no hobos.

She went down the steps with great bravado, but as she neared the place where she and Josh had encountered the two young hobos, she slowed. She shivered in the hot sun and stopped. Then she thought of Oscar . . . and Friday. She slipped aside into the underbrush and went toward WATER BUG. It loomed before her, and she started to climb, zig-zagging up, pulling back every branch.

The rock! But it wasn't the right one. Sweat soaked her shirt, she sneezed. But she kept on searching, ever closer to the hobo camp. She shook her head and whispered fiercely, "I'm not afraid . . . I'm not a sissy." But her mouth tasted like old leaves.

Another rock! No, wrong again. Where *was* it? She stood very still, straining her ears toward the trestle. A train whistle echoed up the valley, and a long freight thundered onto the high trestle. She began to search frantically. She crawled, she yanked branches, she slid, she groaned. Tears welled up in her eyes, her nose dripped. Why hadn't she paid more attention that day she'd found HALL?

The train rumbled away, and she leaned against a big maple tree. She could see smoke rising from a fire in the hobo camp, and then there came bursts of loud laughter. Fearfully she pulled on the limb of the nearest evergreen. A half-shriek came from her throat.

There it was! She ducked under the limb, eased around the rock, and wriggled into the little opening. Panting, she sprawled on the drift of leaves just inside the entrance, listening for sounds of pursuit. But none came and gradually her panting subsided. Her eyes adjusted to the gloom, and she began to look around. The opening was like a porthole in the side of a ship, and the tunnel that led back into WATER BUG was low and narrow. It was filled with wet leaves and pine needles. The side of the HALL was clay, shiny with moisture. Crawly things . . . snakes . . . Kate shook her head. She straightened up, but her head and shoulders scraped the top of the tunnel. She took a few hunched steps over the slimy leaves into the semidarkness.

"Ouch." Her head bumped into something. She reached up and felt wood. She moved her hand along the wood, and a splinter jabbed her big finger. "Ouch," she said again. She popped her finger into her mouth, sucking on it.

What time was it? Would Oscar be in the pines? He'd want to be in on all the first exploring. . . . Relief and dread rippled through her as she turned with only one backward glance at the unknown blackness and crept out under the evergreen limb. Best to explore with Oscar, for he seemed to know about everything.

The warm summer air welcomed her, and she smiled up at the sun sparkling through the screen of leaves far above. She looked about memorizing the surroundings. Three tall maple trees in a V, a big outcropping of rock, and one evergreen that was taller than all the others on WATER BUG. But to make sure she put two sticks in an X at the base of the tree. Then, silent as an Indian, she went up WATER BUG. At the top she marked the spot with another X made from two twigs. She backed away from the edge of WATER BUG fearful that a hobo might be following, but once out of earshot she leaped across the pasture, so happy with herself that she felt as if she could fly. She'd done it; all alone, her fear of hobos notwithstanding.

"TOAD HALL completed," she yelled to the grazing cows as she flew past. She hurried noisily to her secret place to wait. She paced about sucking her finger, so pleased with herself that she couldn't read. "Come, Oscar," she commanded, staring through the pines at the mansion on the hill. "I can't wait to tell you."

She waited and waited.

A watched pot never boils.

She forced herself to pick up a book and open it to the map of the routes of the Underground Railroad. The spiderweb of lines running across the map all ended at one of the lake ports: Sandusky, Cleveland, Painesville, Geneva, Ashtabula. . . .

"Hey, you're here," Oscar said. Kate sprang up.

"Guess what, M'LORD?" She held out her finger with the splinter.

"What?"

"I've found HALL, M'LORD," she said trying to become as calm and collected as Oscar. "See, HALL has wooden beams."

For an instant bewilderment clouded his face. "HALL, HALL. TOAD HALL is over." She danced before him poking her splinter into his face.

"TOAD HALL is over?" he yelled. "Over? Really?"

"Really, truly, cross my heart and hope to die. I just went down WATER BUG and found HALL."

"You're positive it's *the* HALL?"

"Of course it's *the* HALL. It's the only HALL on WATER BUG. There are lots of HALLS out in the lake bluffs; everybody knows about them. Dad's even gone exploring with us through some of the lake HALLS, but I've never heard a single soul say there're HALLS along WATER BUG."

"Jumping Jehosaphat!" Oscar yelled, his calm shattered. "You say there are wooden beams?" He seized her finger and looked at the splinter. Then he let her hand drop, shook off his crutches, grabbed her shoulder, and hobbled about the little clearing. "It doesn't hurt a bit." But he gritted his teeth as he spoke. "That doctor can go to Hades. Get ROSE." He snatched up his discarded crutches and swung toward WATER BUG while she flew to the barn. They met down in the pasture, and Kate led him to the X.

"Down there," she said very softly. Oscar's fingers were shaking so with anticipation that he could hardly tie ROSE around the tree. Kate tied the other end around his middle and hid his crutches under a bush just over the rim of WATER BUG. "We have to be awfully quiet," she whispered. "The hobo camp is right *there*." She pointed almost directly below but off to the left a little.

Oscar nodded. He backed down WATER BUG on his knees, holding onto ROSE. Kate slid down beside him. After a slow, quiet-as-possible descent they reached the tree and the twig X. "There," Kate whispered. She pulled aside the limb, and the rock and the concealed entrance were revealed. Oscar tried to untie himself and look into HALL all at once. Kate wriggled in, and he came crawling after her.

"Crumb," Kate said in a normal tone, sure the hobos couldn't hear her now. "We didn't bring our exploring things."

"Talk soft." Oscar put his finger across his lips. "Loud noises can cause cave-ins."

"HALL-ins," Kate reminded him. Oscar looked keenly into the semidarkness around him. The clay sides and roof of the tunnel oozed water, and the floor was covered with decaying leaves and pine needles that had blown or fallen in the hole. Thoughts of what things might be lurking underfoot evaporated from Kate's head now that Oscar was with her.

"Where are the wooden beams?" They hunched

over and went a few steps, then Kate reared up. She felt along the low roof.

"Here's one." Oscar stuck out his hand and felt the beam. It went across the roof and down either side.

"It's like a support in a mine shaft," Oscar said. Kate stepped out ahead of him.

"Here's another one," she said and then a little later, "and another one."

"Stop, Kate. We gotta have candles," Oscar whispered as loudly as he dared. "We gotta test the air or we could die in here."

"Really die?" Kate asked softly. Their whispers hissed in the eerie half-light. Oscar turned and made his way reluctantly toward the entrance. He squirmed out, blinking at the sudden brightness. Kate didn't want to leave HALL now that Oscar was with her, but she followed slowly. They went back up WATER BUG without speaking, Oscar pulling himself up ROSE, hand over hand, and Kate scrambling beside him.

"Your cast is filthy," she pointed. Oscar looked down. Dirt, soggy leaves, pine needles and small twigs clung to the damp plaster.

"Dead giveaway. I'll get something to wrap it in." He rubbed the dirt from his bare knees and cast as best he could. "Wish I had some old overalls like yours." He looked at Kate's faded ones.

"Mom just put some stuff out for the Goodwill. I'll look in the bag and maybe there're some overalls of Nathan's you can wear," Kate said. They hid ROSE under a bush and went back to the pines talking all the way about the strange hole that was more like a mine shaft than a cave.

They entered their secret place and began to revise their list of needs.

"You have flashlight, candles, knife and water . . . and sweater," Oscar added the last, "and I have candles, matches, string and . . . food." He rubbed his stomach. "We'll have a feast down in HALL." They looked at each other and grinned. Had they forgotten anything? "TOAD HALL completed, M'LADY, thanks to you," Oscar said bowing low. Kate returned the bow. "Meet you here at two sharp," he said. Kate set an imaginary wristwatch. "You're swell, Kate, and it's a swell HALL," Oscar threw over his shoulder as he swung off into the pines.

She didn't touch the ground all the way to the house. As she charged across the yard and took the two steps to the side porch in one leap, Margaret looked up from her solitary game of jacks. "Got ants in your pants?"

"Dry up." Kate slowed a bit, but once out of Margaret's sight she took the front stairs two at a time to her room. She'd gotten a flashlight to take to Y camp last summer, and she dug it out from the bottom of her little cedar chest where she kept her clean hankies and stuck it under her pillow. Then she tiptoed down the hall to Nathan and Josh's room. She peeped in, then sneaked to the closet door. As she opened it, the putrid smell of Josh's feet burst out. She held her nose. The floor was ankle deep in shoes, dirty clothes, balled-up socks and dust. Nathan's high-top boots tilted crazily in the back corner. Attached to the side of the left boot was a knife holder and inside it was Nathan's Boy Scout knife. She eased it from its little pocket, backed out over the debris and bumped squarely into Margaret.

"That's Nathan's knife," she pointed accusingly.

"He said I could use it." Kate went out of the room, Margaret on her heels. Kate whirled on her. "I'll read *Peter Rabbit* to you." Margaret didn't budge.

"I'm going to tell Nathan."

"Tell him then, see if I care," Kate shrugged. Margaret's interest crumbled.

"Read *Peter* to me?"

"Said I would," Kate yelled. Margaret ran down the stairs to find the worn book in the bookcase. Kate rushed into her room, hid the knife with the flashlight and raced after Margaret. She read *Peter Rabbit* five times in a row, mouthing the familiar phrases, her mind on HALL.

"It was nice of you to read to Margaret," Mom said, fanning with her cardboard funeral fan as they sat down for lunch.

"Where's Josh?" Kate asked.

"Collecting for the *Ladies Home Journal*. And Simone went with him." Mom shook her head in wonder. "Never thought I'd see the day when Josh played with a girl."

"Simone's more like a boy than a girl," Margaret said.

"She certainly is a tomboy." Mom laughed. "She jumped off the garage-shed roof before I could stop her, but I scolded her for fair. If anything else happens to those two while they're on this property, I'll just die. By the way, how's Oscar? Have you seen him lately?"

"Not lately," Kate said. "Lately" she interpreted as meaning five minutes ago.

"Wonder how he's getting along?" Mom said.

Lunch was over quickly, and Kate read *Peter* twice more to Margaret. She wanted her to forget about the knife. In spite of the heat Margaret sat cuddled against her on the lumpy couch. Finally she fell asleep.

Mom was napping upstairs. Kate eased herself from the couch, sneaked into the pantry and got an empty canning jar, which she filled with water. Quietly she opened the door of the old oak sideboard in the dining room and took some candle stubs from Mom's emergency box. Then she crept upstairs and got the knife and the flashlight, and grabbed her oldest sweater from the bottom of her drawer. All these items fitted easily into her sling. On her way out she searched the Goodwill bag on the front porch. She found a threadbare pair of Nathan's overalls, patched many times at the knees and seat, which she also stuffed into her sling. After collecting the water jar and candles, she looked around the deserted yard and went by a circuitous route, afraid that Josh and Simone might have returned and be spying on her. She didn't want them to see her now that she and Oscar were on the point of real discovery.

Oscar was late, but at last he came struggling into the clearing dragging a bag. Kate tossed the discarded overalls to him. They had to use the knife to slit the leg so he could get his cast in, but otherwise they fit loosely over his blue shorts. He had come with a dish towel over his cast, held in place with red rubber bands.

"Ready?" Kate stood up eagerly.

"On to HALL." Oscar started forward on his crutches. Kate grabbed the bag, stuffed her items into it and swung it over her shoulder. They hurried to WATER BUG and went down ROSE. They pulled the limb back and crawled in on all fours. It smelled like the inside of a rotting log. Kate shivered, remembering her first fears about snakes and crawly things. She hunched into herself, trying not to touch anything.

Oscar paused, dug into the bag and came out with a box of candles and matches. He lit the candle and watched its steady glow.

"Good," he said. Kate also lighted a candle. That was better, she thought, or was it worse . . . now that she'd be able to see the crawly things . . .

"We know that this air near the entrance is OK," Oscar said, thrusting his candle in every direction. "But from here on, we've got to be very, very careful."

"Careful of what exactly?" Kate asked peering all about.

"Poisoned air. If the candle burns bright and straight, it's OK. Too bad we don't have a canary. Miners used to take canaries in little cages to test the air. If the canary died, the miners scrammed out of that tunnel or shaft or whatever they were in . . . fast."

"If the canary died . . ." Kate hated anything to be hurt.

"Better the canary than the miners," Oscar said practically. "Anyway, even though people have suffocated in caves and old mine shafts, Cripples Incorporated can't stop now."

"Right." Kate shivered happily. With Oscar here, the danger seemed alluring.

"And HALL-ins. The least little thing can cause one, so watch out." He began to creep forward slowly, so slowly that Kate fidgeted. They passed huge clumps of clay that had fallen into the passageway between the supporting beams. They moved awkwardly holding convulsively to their candles.

Kate got ahead of Oscar. He was examining every wooden arch and HALL-in personally. Kate tried to wait for him, but she just couldn't. She pushed ahead into the darkness. Oscar could tell by her stiff back that she was mad.

"Come on, Kate, be a sport," he whispered urgently. "I'm not being slow just to be slow. We just have to be sensible, that's all."

"Sensible." Kate whirled. "You're being so sensible we'll *never* get HALL explored."

"Sure we will," Oscar said gently. "Can't help it if I know all the things that can happen in HALLS."

Kate glared at him. "It's my Secret, my HALL and I'm going to explore it any way I want, sensible or not. You can come if you're not too sensible . . . or scared by all that dumb reading you've done about dead canaries and heartless miners."

Oscar hobbled after her meekly waving his candle about.

HALL's opening had been torturously small, but after they had gone a few yards the passage leading back into WATER BUG widened and got taller. Kate stood up, feeling above her with her hands so she wouldn't bump her head again. Slowly they made their way over the slippery floor. In spite of herself Kate lagged. She waited for Oscar now, and they moved together. Then something loomed up ahead.

"I told you so," Oscar gloated, pointing to the wall of rocks blocking their way. "A real big HALL-in." Kate didn't utter a word, and she hoped Oscar couldn't hear her heart jumping about in her chest. Laboriously he pulled himself up the pile. He moved his candle about just below the top of the passage where the stones were wedged together. "Well, that's the end of our exploring," he called down softly. "This HALL-in fills the entire passage."

"Really?" Kate said, her disappointment immense within her.

Oscar came down very slowly. He sat on a big rock at the bottom and set his candle on a flat stone. "This tunnel is definitely man-made . . . dug out with a pick or something."

"And these beams didn't grow in here like trees," Kate said. They sat in the glow of their candles, looking up and down the shaft. Several silent minutes passed. Then Kate grabbed the bag, dug about in it and drew out her flashlight. She shined it along the walls. "Can't be a real mine shaft, though," Kate said. "Nothing to mine around here—no coal or . . ."

"Then who dug it, and why?" Oscar mused.

"Think it's part of the Secret?" Kate asked, squatting on her haunches and continuing her flashlight investigation.

"Don't know." Oscar shook his head, puzzled. They sat speculating for a long time. Then Oscar said, "Teatime." He hobbled to the bag and dug about, until he brought out a cardboard box and the ritual began. He untied it, lifted off the lid, unfolded the white linen napkin that was tucked around the contents and spread it on the rock nearest him. Then he unwrapped the waxed paper bundle and laid dainty white triangular sandwiches without crusts in a precise row on the napkin-tablecloth. Next he unwrapped oatmeal cookies and arranged them in an overlapping circle. Finally with a bow, he handed an embroidered linen napkin to Kate and said, "Tea is served, M'LADY."

"But there's no tea!" Kate exclaimed.

"Who cares," Oscar laughed. "Never drink the stuff anyway. Tea is goodies, not tea at all." He picked up a sandwich and bit it daintily in two. Kate pried open the tiny white triangle.

"Cucumber," she marveled, "and what's that green stuff?"

"Watercress." Kate burst out laughing. Oscar Watercress Witherspoon.

"Do you have tea every day?" she asked.

"Every day," Oscar said. "Tea at four and dinner at eight-thirty."

"We eat at five-thirty on the dot when Dad and Nathan get home. They're hungry then." Kate knew what Dad would think of these thin cucumber and watercress sandwiches. He had three thick sand-

wiches with crusts as a starter for lunch.

"I love tea," Oscar said. He rubbed his stomach.

"So do I," Kate said liking what he liked. "Josh would be green if he could see me now." She stretched contentedly.

"Simone, too," Oscar chuckled. "She'll be sorry she was so snotty about this." He stuck out his cast. "She's always blowing off about Josh-this and Josh-that. Makes me sick. But once they see that Cripples Incorporated has solved the Secret of the Strawbridge Place, then they'll wish they'd been nicer . . ."

The flashlight dimmed dangerously. Kate flicked it off and only their two candles glowed. "Tea by candlelight." Oscar crooked his little finger as he selected a cookie. He ate one after another, and Kate lost count after eleven.

A disk of pale light was visible at the end of the tunnel. "Takes nourishment to solve secrets . . . brain food. We'll bring more supplies each time we come and then we'll have plenty in case of an emergency."

They stored their things in the empty tea box, crawled to the entrance, and Oscar stuck his head out. He looked warily up and down the valley and listened before he emerged into the stifling afternoon heat. Kate followed. Oscar pulled himself up ROSE on his knees, and Kate made her way clumsily beside him. With Oscar beside her, the threat of the hobo camp receded.

They hid ROSE, Nathan's overalls and the dish towel and rubber bands in the same bush where Oscar had hidden his crutches.

"Tomorrow in the pines as early as you can, and we'll look in HALL again," Oscar said retrieving his crutches. "Mom comes back on Friday, so we haven't much time." He took the bag and swung away toward their secret place, his head down, watching for cow patches.

As she set the table for supper that evening Kate said, "Mom, I need more batteries for my flashlight."

"Are you reading under the covers again?" Mom looked at her sharply. "You know it's bad for your eyes."

"No, I'm not reading. The light is just getting dim, and I'll need it for Y camp."

"There won't be any Y camp this year," Mom sighed. She shook her head in a weary way. Kate made a face. Those hard times again.

Supper was promptly at five-thirty. It was meat loaf. Josh and Nathan had four helpings. Kate had only one because she was still full from tea.

# Chapter 7

As early as you can Oscar had said, but Kate knew that quarter after five was too early even for Oscar. Nevertheless, she tiptoed down the bare back stairs carrying her old sneakers. Blackie meowed outside. Kate unhooked the screen and sniffed the cool morning air as Blackie humped against her legs. Mom and Dad always left all the doors and windows open so that the night air could circulate through the old house. Poor Mom, hot weather frazzled her.

Kate fed Blackie, then helped herself to more candles from the emergency box in the sideboard. Mom wouldn't miss these stubs, there were too many in the box. She hid them under the grapevine that sprawled over the slanted cellar doors. The stone porch felt good on her bare feet.

The clock said twenty-seven after five. Kate glared up at it, willing it forward. She couldn't wait to see Oscar again. To help pass the interminable time she started breakfast. She measured coffee into the top of the old percolator, filled it with water and set it over the gas burner. When Mom came down yawning and rubbing her eyes, the aroma filled the kitchen. "My magic helper," Mom said kissing her sleepily. She patted Kate's cast. "Hurt?"

"Not any more."

"That's nice." Mom poured a cup of coffee and drank, struggling to wake up. But Kate felt vibrant.

Breakfast was in slow motion. She played with her cereal and nibbled on her toast, her stomach heaving. Finally she couldn't force any more down, and she put her dishes in the sink. She stood poised at the screen door. "Where to?" Mom looked up.

"To read in my place in the pines. What else can I do with this?" Kate stuck out her cast. Mom nodded absently. Kate slipped out. She retrieved the candle stubs and raced away from the house.

Oscar came sooner than she had expected. She jumped to greet him. He rushed in on his crutches and spilled the contents of the bag that he carried over his shoulder into the clearing. Out rolled three boxes of candles, two flashlights, batteries, matches, two cans of pork and beans, a can of black olives, two spoons, a can opener, paper napkins and a large tea box securely tied with a string.

"That's a bigger tea box than yesterday," he said proudly.

"On to HALL," said Kate. They gathered up all the things, plus the books they had left on the ground yesterday, dumped them helter-skelter into the bag and hurried off through the pasture to the place where ROSE was hidden. Oscar pulled on Nathan's overalls and snapped the rubber bands over the towel that Kate had wrapped around his cast. They descended stealthily and entered HALL. Using their flashlights, they went past the clay HALL-ins to the rock HALL-in.

Oscar settled himself and again upset the bag. Cans and books, candles and can openers spilled out. Oscar gathered up the books and shoved two at Kate. Then suddenly he became still and let his head loll back on his shoulders in a relaxed way. Slowly he began to rotate his head, round once, twice, three times. . . .

"What *are* you doing?" Kate demanded. Oscar didn't answer, just continued his strange head maneuvers. He seemed to be in a trance. "Oscar," Kate said in her most disgusted voice. "*What are you doing?*" He put his finger to his lips and went on rotating his head like a zombie.

Kate gave him a look of complete contempt, and taking her flashlight shined the beam over the walls and ceiling of the tunnel. The heavy supports still stood stolidly, and between some there were wooden panels to hold back the dirt walls. Just beside the rock HALL-in was a long panel that was three times as wide as a door. Kate got up and looked at it more closely. Then she turned the flashlight on the opposite wall. There were no corresponding wooden panels there. There had never been any panels there, for the wall was pockmarked with small holes where the clay had fallen away. Whoever built this shaft didn't do the same thing on both sides.

"Funny," she said under her breath, turning back to the paneled wall.

"What's funny?" Oscar asked coming out of his trance.

"Well, it's about time," Kate said. "What was all that about anyway?"

"Letting myself go empty so I could be open to the spirits of this place and maybe feel what went on here."

"You're nuts," Kate said.

"No, I'm not," Oscar said evenly. "Sometimes when you make yourself receptive, your mind absorbs things you can't explain rationally."

"Gee whiz," Kate said sarcastically, but she couldn't stay angry with Oscar. "Look, Oscar, these walls don't match." She shined the flashlight on one, then the other.

"Uh . . . huh," Oscar said following the flashlight's quick movements.

"Do you think it could be a clue?"

"Maybe."

"Didn't your spirits give you any clues about this tunnel?" Kate asked.

Oscar crawled to the paneled wall. He started at the left side and began to examine the panels closely with his flashlight. An inch at a time he went up the sides to the low ceiling and then down again. Kate watched a while, then flipped open one of the books. She began reading words, sentences, but they didn't go together. She tossed the book aside and crawled over to the right edge of the panel and began examining it much as Oscar was. They worked in silence. Kate was the first to give up. "This isn't any fun," she said. "Let's do something else." Oscar didn't stop or turn.

"Detective work is mostly dull," he said.

"How do you know? You ever been a detective?"

"No, but I've read lots of detective stories. And clues don't just happen. You have to find them; and once you find them, you have to put them together so they make some sort of sense."

Kate sniffed and crawled forward toward the entrance. She blinked at the brightness. She could see nothing except the light; everything around the entrance looked obscure and black. She didn't want to go out and leave Oscar, so she knelt a few feet from the light and shined her flashlight around the entrance.

She gasped, edged forward, put out her hand, felt

the handle on the door that appeared to the left side of the entrance hole.

"Oscar!" she wispered urgently. "Oscar!"

"What?"

"Come here . . . quick." He came. Kate pointed with the flashlight beam.

"I'll be a son of a gun," Oscar said. They both began feeling the door all over, shining their flashlights on it. Oscar stuck his head out the hole they had come through. "The dirt's worn away here along the door frame and made the hole we came in, but the door is the original exit. This dirt fell in because there was nothing behind it to support it."

"So our hole isn't supposed to be there at all," Kate breathed.

"No," Oscar said. "This door is the exit." They crouched before it looking at it in wonder.

"This puts a whole new light on things," Oscar said, slowly withdrawing so they wouldn't be talking so close to the opening. Now Kate stuck close beside him.

"What do you mean . . . a whole new light on things?" she asked.

"Fairies didn't put that door there, Kate. People did."

"But what people . . . and why?"

"That's what you and I have to figure out. But someone put that door there, someone dug this tunnel, someone put up these supporting beams, someone used this tunnel for something . . ."

"But WHAT?" Kate exploded. Oscar didn't answer immediately. Then he asked.

"Kate, you ever play down there along the river?"

"Sure."

"Ever see anything peculiar down there?"

"Peculiar how?"

"Come on, Kate. I've got to see something." He was up and hurried toward the entrance.

Bewildered and half-angry, Kate followed him. They listened, then eased themselves out the hole and slid down the short distance to the valley floor. Oscar grabbed Kate's shoulder and hobbled beside her as they went toward the river. Kate kept looking over her shoulder toward the hobo camp, but soon they were out of earshot. They came to the edge of the river. Oscar began peering along the muddy edge. He pushed Kate in his excitement. "Hey, don't shove so hard. What are you so all fired up about anyway?"

"You ever remember any dock along here, Kate?"

"Nope."

"Nothing at all. Even the ruin of a dock . . . like a timber or an old rotting platform? . . ."

"Nope."

"You sure?"

"Sure I'm sure. I've lived here all my life, haven't

I, and I've been along this bank about a million times, so there."

Oscar leaned against a big tree trunk, a discouraged look settling over his face. His shoulders slumped. "Well, that blows that theory."

"What theory?"

"I thought maybe the tunnel was the hiding place for the slaves, and then they were rowed down the river. They would have had to have been smuggled aboard the lake boats at night when no one was watching 'cause black people couldn't just walk onto a boat big as life and ride to Canada like white folks."

"Why, I never thought of that," Kate said. "Wonder if they wore disguises?"

"Must have. The slave owners sent spies up north to watch likely spots where the slaves would have to come. But where are the clothes? Nothing in that tunnel that I saw."

"We haven't really looked," Kate said, forgetting that only half an hour ago she'd been bored with the tunnel. "Come on, Oscar, maybe there's more up there than meets the eye."

They rushed back through the underbrush and up WATER BUG, too excited to be cautious. They tumbled into the narrow entrance, taking a large section of dirt with them. The entrance suddenly yawned twice as large and gaped below the evergreen limb. But they were too busy to notice. They seized their abandoned flashlights. "You take that side; I'll take this," Oscar said. They shined the beams over the dripping clay walls, the stout timbers. They ran their hands over the beams. They worked their way back toward the rock HALL-in.

"It's just the same old smelly tunnel," Kate said, collapsing after an hour's fruitless searching. Oscar was still feeling the panels that were on his side of the tunnel. When she spoke, he stopped and hobbled down beside her. He looked at his watch.

"It's almost noon. I've got to go home to lunch or Maida'll think I've been kidnapped, and she'll send the sheriff out after me."

"I gotta go too," Kate said. They got up and made their way up ROSE to the pasture. They left the overalls, cast towel and rubber bands in the bushes, then walked across the pasture, washed as best they could in the old bathtub that served as a watering trough for the cows and horses, and turned to look at each other.

"Shall we go back to HALL this afternoon?" Kate asked.

"Sure. We have lots more exploring to do in there." They parted, Oscar swinging out eagerly toward the mansion. He seemed on fire about the tunnel.

Kate watched him go, but she felt none of his

enthusiasm. She shuddered at the thought of returning to that ugly hole where no matter how hard they searched, they found nothing. Of course, she'd found the door, but. . . . She climbed up the wooden gate, sat on the top, and thought over the events of the morning. Despair, hope, excitement, frustration . . . she pouted. Oscar didn't make up for the fact that she wasn't becoming Ashtabula's sidestroke champion, but she had to admit that Cripples Incorporated was better than nothing. Then Mom called, "Kate, Josh, Margaret, lunch." And she jumped down from the gate and hurried toward the house.

# Chapter 8

Josh and Margaret had to do the lunch dishes because Mom went to lie down. Kate escaped the house and went to the pines. Oscar was already there. They went without a word across the pasture and got ready to descend WATER BUG. They went down, and as they neared HALL, they could hear angry voices coming from the hobo camp. They flopped in the entrance in a hurry. "Hey." Oscar pointed. "That's a lot bigger than it was."

"Yeah." Kate looked hard at the opening. "We're knocking the dirt away when we crawl in and out. Maybe we should fill it in and use the door?" They looked out the hole. The door was camouflaged with dirt and leaves and twigs. "But if we scrape off the door and use it, it'll be visible and anyone could find it."

"We have to use the hole," Oscar said. He pressed some of the dirt back into the opening. "We'll build it up each time we leave. Come on, Kate, all during lunch I kept thinking about those panels back next to the rock HALL-in. Why aren't there panels on both sides?"

"Yeah," Kate said knowingly, but really she didn't know at all.

He crawled away, and Kate followed, shivering in the wet smelly gloom. Her sweater lay discarded near the bag, and she pulled it on. It had a huge hole in one elbow and there were only three buttons. She joined Oscar who was continuing his inch-by-inch scrutiny of the panels. Taking her flashlight she shined the beam on the wall, probing along the very top of the rock pile, then gradually she lowered it along the uneven edge. The panels went behind the rocks. She got up, stuck her flashlight in her overall's pocket and began pushing at the rocks of the HALL-in. They cascaded down, clattering and bumping.

"You gone mad or something? Want the roof to HALL-in on us?" Oscar whispered severely. Involuntarily they both looked up and held their flashlights to the roof.

There were no rocks along the roof!

They stared. No rocks. No rocks in the ceiling of the tunnel. Oscar kept staring up at the ceiling from which no rocks could have fallen to make the rock HALL-in, but Kate came alive. She rushed back to the panels that extended behind the rocks. How far back did the wooden panels go? Crash, bang, bump, rattle, thump . . . the rocks spun down, pushed by Kate's frantic hands. Oscar still stared at the ceiling.

"Kate, you nut, stop. . . ." Oscar began. But Kate paid no attention. She seized her flashlight and scanned the newly bared wall. A shadow leaped at her. She held it in the beam as she clambered up the cold stones.

"Oscar," she breathed. "Look what I found."

"What?" he asked coming out of his ceiling-staring pose.

"Look." She waggled her flashlight on the wall. He was beside her, dragging his heavy cast over her foot, bumping into her. "It's a bolt," she said.

"Well, I'll be . . ."

"And there's a crack all up and down, and the bolt goes across it." Kate used her flashlight to show him.

Oscar stuck his nose right into the wall, then he reared back fingering the bolt. It was rusty and corroded.

"Kate, you're terrific. How'd you know where to look?"

"The spirits of the tunnel spoke to me," she said.

"Oh, you. . . . But so what? Who cares how you found it, it's found. Let's get these rocks away and try to open that door."

In a fever of excitement, they began to cast rocks away. A half-hour's steady work finally revealed all

84

the door from ceiling to floor. Oscar began to work the bolt. It didn't want to move, but he took Nathan's Boy Scout knife and pried the knob up, then worked it back and forth until it slid a little. At last he shot it back with a grinding rusty bang. "There." He pulled. Nothing moved. He pushed. The panel creaked inward. He grabbed his flashlight and stuck it in. A passageway loomed around the HALL-in.

"It's a bypass, Kate." He stepped inside, holding the door at first. Then he knelt, seized a rock, propped the door open, got a second rock and put it by the first, before he stepped into the corridor and disappeared.

"Wait." Kate dropped her flashlight, grabbed up the bag, and climbed over the scattered rocks to the bypass door. "We gotta test the air, Oscar. Wait, Oscar." She searched frantically and finally her fingers found a candle and matches. She lighted it, watched it glow steadily, then she stepped into the bypass.

Oscar was just a blur of bobbing light ahead. Kate hurried after him, paying no attention to the corridor. She ran a little, keeping Oscar's flashlight in sight. But suddenly the light ahead went out.

"Oscar," Kate wailed. "Wait for me."

The light appeared as suddenly as it had vanished. Oscar's voice came echoing down the corridor. "Kate, wait till you see *this*." She ran ahead, the bag bumping against her legs. Oscar's light had disappeared again. She came to a sharp bend, turned around it, and saw Oscar standing ahead of her. He held out his hand and grabbed her cast. "Come here, Kate, look what I found." They edged around an outcropping of rock that seemed to block the corridor, squeezed through a narrow opening, then Oscar flicked on his flashlight.

"Oh, oh, Oscar," Kate gasped, "it can't be."

"But it is," Oscar gloated. "It's an honest-to-goodness, natural HALL, not a tunnel or a shaft or anything made with a pick. It's a real HALL."

"Like the HALLS that Dad took us into out along the lake bluffs." Kate couldn't believe her eyes.

"Are there other HALLS around Ashtabula?" Oscar demanded.

"Sure, that's what I'm telling you. But they're all out along the lake bluffs. No one's ever found any HALLS this far inland."

Oscar grabbed her shoulder in his frenzy. "Kate, it's all beginning to connect. This HALL and the tunnel to the edge of WATER BUG. . . ."

"Connect how?"

"Don't you see. Here's a natural HALL. A manmade tunnel leads from it to WATER BUG. Grand River flows right along there. It must have something to do with the slaves and the Secret. It's too logical to have just happened."

86

Kate's legs wobbled and she sat down abruptly.

"We've got to explore here, Kate. Maybe there are more tunnels connecting more natural HALLS and more exits and . . ." He limped away toward the nearest wall, probing it with his flashlight beam.

"Hold on, Oscar. The canary's dying."

"What?" Oscar stopped in his tracks. He dragged his cast over to her. They stared at the candle flame. It wavered, grew tall and lean, smoked a little. The smoke drifted toward the passage they had just come down.

"A bit of air movement." Oscar sounded very scientific, then he wet his finger and stuck it straight up. Kate couldn't help giggling. "Cross ventilation," Oscar muttered. "It must be that there's a second entrance somewhere in this HALL. Come on, Kate, search. We're on the verge of something terrific. Can't you feel it?"

"Yeah." Oscar's excitement was infectious.

This HALL wasn't wet and slimy as the tunnel had been. Layers of rock formed the ceiling and walls, and small stones and boulders covered the floor. Oscar was already at the wall, shooting his flashlight beam about. Kate shrugged the bag to the floor, set the candle down between two rocks, and reached into her pocket for her flashlight. "Rats," she said rising. She'd left it back in the tunnel. She went to get it and was back before Oscar realized she was missing.

Settling the candle between two rocks again, she went toward the wall opposite Oscar. Her foot slipped and she fell forward, her cast cracking loudly.

"Help me!" she yelled. Oscar swung his flashlight beam toward her.

"Oh," he said. Kate twisted around to look at the spot where his flashlight beam had stopped.

"Oh," she said just as Oscar had. Simultaneously they crept toward the disk of light and the object resting there. They came together, knelt, and stared down into the middle of the circle of light.

"What is it?" Oscar asked.

"Looks like a box," Kate answered reaching out and touching it tentatively.

"What's it doing here in the middle of HALL?"

"Maybe it has something to do with the Secret," Kate said as she began to lift it.

"Don't move it," Oscar said sternly. Kate reared back.

"Why not?"

"Might be an important clue. Let's just look at it a bit." They squatted, training both their flashlights on the box. It was about two feet long, about ten inches wide, was hinged in the back and had a lock on the front. There was a metal handle on the top.

"It's locked," Kate said.

"Must have something valuable in it to be locked."

"I want to pick it up, Oscar," Kate said.

"Not yet. Let's look about here a bit." They examined the floor, but found nothing. Finally Oscar returned to the box and squatted before it again. He touched it, ran his hand over it.

"It's my box," Kate warned. "I get to open it." Oscar pulled his hand back. Kate lifted the box into her lap. She shook it once, then let it fall onto the stones beside her. Oscar picked it up and shook it again. He held it to his ear. "Nothing rattles."

"It's empty," Kate said unhappily.

"Why lock it if it's empty? Let's look for a key." They crept over the stony floor with their flashlights, but again they found nothing. "Guess we'll have to break it open. We'll take it up when we go and open it tomorrow. But right now it's teatime," Oscar said.

They lighted two more candles. Oscar used the box as a tea table. He covered it with the napkin and spread the feast. Kate's stomach rumbled as she reached for the crustless triangle sandwiches. They were cucumber and watercress again. She chewed happily. "Oscar, Cripples Incorporated isn't doing badly at all, is it?"

He grinned, his mouth too full to answer.

After tea they examined the walls of the HALL again, but at quarter to five Oscar signaled they should stop. They left their books, candles, everything that had been in the bag and put the box into the bag. Kate swung it over her shoulder. They made their way out the bypass, removed the stones, closed and bolted the door and went out the cold, slippery tunnel.

Smoke was rising from the fire in the hobo camp. They crept out the opening, shoved dirt, leaves and pine needles to build it up again as best they could, then they pulled themselves up ROSE. Once at the top

Oscar wriggled out of Nathan's overalls and the cover for his cast. "Tomorrow as early as you can in the pines, and we'll open the box first thing," Oscar said taking the bag from Kate's shoulder. "Hey, Kate, you still got your sweater on." She looked down, then stripped it off and tossed it under the bush with the overalls.

"Tomorrow," she said. She held out her hand, and Oscar shook it. "Cripples Incorporated, onward," Kate said, then turned and raced across the pasture shouting, "Tomorrow, tomorrow, tomorrow," all the time waving back at Oscar.

# Chapter 9

When Kate came to the screen door, Dad and Nathan were already home and the picnic hamper was on the table. Mom was humming. Something wrapped in a big white tea towel rested on the table. Kate rattled the door. Mom smiled as she unhooked it. "Well, hello there, stranger. Where've you been all afternoon?"

"Reading."

"Reading, Kate?" Mom stood, her arms akimbo on her hips. "Then how did you get so filthy?"

Kate looked down at herself in surprise. Her overalls were wet and muddy, even her cast was dirty.

"Must have been a dirty book." Mom smiled at her own joke.

"Hey, Mom, isn't *Little Women* the grandest book ever, huh, Mom?" Kate rushed in. Mom's stiff elbows collapsed, and she tousled Kate's disheveled hair.

"Go wash." She turned back to the refrigerator and took out two jars of freshly squeezed orange juice. Kate smacked her lips. She reached out a grubby hand and lifted the dish towel. There lay a flat chocolate cake with Mom's special fudge icing.

"Chocolate cake and orange juice," she yelled rushing up the back stairs. It was a special, special picnic when Mom baked a cake.

They drove to the lake, the hamper on the floor of the front seat before Kate and Margaret. Mom, sitting between Nathan and Josh, fanned in the back seat with her cardboard funeral fan.

"Nathan put on his first carburetor today . . . all by himself," Dad boasted. "Didn't you, son?"

"Yeah."

"He's a real help down there. Don't know how I ever got along without him!"

"Can't I help you too, Dad?" Josh leaned forward and breathed on Dad's neck.

"Grow some, squirt, and you can," Dad chuckled. Josh slumped back, stuck his elbow out the open window and frowned. Kate felt sorry for him for the first time since she'd broken her arm. He despised his smallness.

Kate waded while the other gamboled about in the water. She helped Margaret build a sand castle for her new paper doll, but her mind flitted between the mysterious box and the cake in the hamper. Then while Margaret was diving off Dad's shoulders in great splashing belly flops, she wandered up toward the bluffs. There were two cave entrances here that she knew about, but there could be more all along the lake cliffs. Were these caves connected in any way to the one she and Oscar had discovered that very afternoon? The Strawbridge Place was only a couple of miles away from the lake edge. . . .

"Kate," Mom called, and she scampered toward the log, kicking the sand high with her heels.

She ate until her stomach was tight and hard. She saved all her icing till the very last, then ate it slowly, holding it as long as she could while it melted under her tongue. When the last sweet taste was gone, she sat up and asked, "Dad, how come those caves are in the cliffs?"

"Don't know, honey. Always been there as far as I know."

"But are these the only caves in Ashtabula?"

"Who knows," Dad shrugged. "This area has the right kind of stone for caves—limestone—but the only caves anyone's ever discovered are these that have entrances here on these bluffs. But that doesn't mean there couldn't be others that no one's ever found."

Kate hugged herself. "Mom, may I have another piece of cake?"

"Of course, honey." The world was suddenly just about perfect.

The next morning Kate was up and away before Mom had her wits about her.

This was the day of the box!

She raced to the pines and stared at the mysterious box. She shook it, looked at it, felt it all over. Oscar came very soon, the bag over his shoulder. He dropped his crutches, reached in and took out a hatchet and a white cardboard box. "How's that?" he asked gleefully, waving the box in her face. "That's the biggest tea box ever."

"The hatchet," Kate demanded. How could Oscar think of food at this momentous moment? He handed it to her without a word. She seized it and began hacking ineptly at the box.

"Here, let me . . ." Oscar said, forgetting himself.

"No." Kate jerked away. "It's *my* box, *my* HALL, *my* Secret, *my* . . ."

" . . . everything," Oscar finished for her. But Kate was too preoccupied to retort. She tried to bash the box in, but it was too strong. She hacked at it, slammed it against a tree, finally threw it to the ground and jumped on it with both feet. But it remained stoutly, solidly, intact. Tears of bafflement rimmed her eyes, and finally she hurled the box at Oscar and threw herself full length on the pine needles and cried.

Oscar took the box. He took the hatchet and began chipping away at the wood around the lock flap.

95

Patiently he worked. His glasses slipped down his nose. Kate propped herself on her good elbow to watch. Finally the lock flap loosened, he pried at it, and it came off. He held the box out to Kate. "You look first . . . it's *your* box." Kate seized it and yanked the lid up.

"It's empty!" she raged throwing it to the ground. Oscar picked it up and looked at it very carefully. They sat for several minutes staring at the vacant wooden interior. At last Kate wiped her nose with the end of Nathan's shirt and sprang up. She'd counted too much on that box's not being empty. "HALL's still there. Come on, Oscar, we have exploring to do."

"Right," he said, but he kept muttering under his breath about anyone crazy enough to lock an empty box. Kate was too angry at the box to listen to him. She shouldered the bag, empty but for the tea box, and together they went across the pasture, descended WATER BUG and entered HALL. They crawled carefully through the crumbling entrance, opened the bypass door, propped it securely with two stones, and hurried down the corridor to the natural HALL. Silently they separated, Oscar beginning to search HALL's wall to the left, Kate searching to the right. Deliberately they moved around the huge dark space, their flashlights probing every crevice and shadow.

An hour passed.

Kate often glanced over at Oscar, but he was doing exactly what she was doing. She trembled in the chill dead air, but she wouldn't pause long enough to get her sweater. She had to beat Oscar at . . . at . . . whatever they were looking for. Rushing ahead, she used her flashlight like a water hose. She stopped at a zigzag in the wall and rested her cast on a convenient ledge. Then raising her flashlight to eye level she shined it into the zigzag.

"Oscar, Oscar . . ." she exulted. "I've found it . . . found it. Come, quick."

"What?" he whispered urgently.

"An exit," Kate whispered back. He was beside her in a minute, and their combined flashlight beams illuminated a natural passageway leading off . . . somewhere.

"Let's go." Oscar pushed forward. They both tried to squeeze into the corridor at once, then Oscar retreated. "It's *your* passageway, you found it." He bowed mockingly. Kate stuck out her tongue and waggled it in his face. "Candles and string." Oscar turned away, pretending he didn't see Kate. Kate watched him, hands on her hips. Didn't anything ever get under his skin?

He got a ball of string, tied one end around a rock and tested it carefully to make sure it couldn't be pulled loose. Then he handed the string ball to Kate, and lighted a candle. "Please, M'LADY, proceed," he said. Kate tossed her head as she stepped before him into the passageway.

The tunnel twisted slowly upward with many smaller passageways leading off on either side. But these corridors were too small to be of any significance, and the two explorers kept to the large main passageway.

"It's like a honeycomb," Oscar said softly looking down one little serpentine tunnel after another.

"A labyrinth," Kate said. They continued down the main corridor for about ten minutes, then they came to a place where the tunnel divided into three major corridors.

"Which way?" Kate asked feeling very sassy since she'd found this new section of HALL.

"The middle corridor might please, M'LADY." Kate at once turned to the right corridor. They followed it for several minutes, Kate letting out the string and Oscar holding the candle. But soon the corridor narrowed, faltered, and ended in a blank wall. They turned around discouraged, and Kate began to gather up the string. "Leave it," Oscar said. "Then we'll know what passages we've explored."

"Why?" Kate asked irritably.

"It's *my* string," Oscar said sarcastically. "And I said leave it." Kate dropped the ball sulkily.

"You're just wasting it," she muttered to the wall.

They retraced their steps. Once back at the place where the corridor divided three ways, they paused. Oscar went back to HALL and got a second ball of string and Nathan's Boy Scout knife. He gave them to Kate. She stuck them in her pocket with her flashlight. Then they turned to the middle branch and were just going to enter it when Oscar stumbled over something. He lowered his candle and peered at it nearsightedly.

"Hey, Kate, look at that. It's another box." Kate pulled her flashlight from her pocket and flicked the little button. The box lay canted on its side, the front end pointing toward the left corridor and the other end pointing down the main corridor that led back to HALL.

"It's exactly like the other one." She knelt beside it, wonderingly. "And it's locked, too."

"And probably empty," Oscar said. "Let's not fight over it. We'll open it when we get through exploring." They abandoned the box, went into the middle corridor, but after half an hour of slow going this corridor ended as abruptly as the first passage had. They retraced their steps and went all the way back to the big HALL and rested, drinking water and having an apple from Oscar's tea box.

"Let's try the last branch," Oscar said. They stuffed more string and candles into their pockets and took the flashlights and set off. They passed the box and headed down the left corridor. The search was again slow, for this tunnel sloped down, and it became wet and the rocks slippery. Oscar went so slowly that Kate had to sit down and wait for him. They were just about to turn back when around a bend they came upon another division in the tunnel. Kate dropped the string ball. Her teeth chattered with the cold. Oscar sank down on a boulder and massaged his leg. Kate took her flashlight from her pocket and began a careful examination of the area. She needed to keep moving if she was going to stay warm. Oscar sat, his head in his hands, breathing hard. Kate's light moved up and down, back and forth, the ceiling, the walls, the floor. . . . She felt the hairs on her neck prickle.

"Oscar . . ." She held the beam steady on the place on the floor. "Look."

He looked, and his hands stopped in midair.

Another box, exactly like the other ones, rested squarely in their path. It was lying on its side, angled toward the left tunnel ahead. "This is getting spooky," Kate whispered.

"Yeah." Oscar stared and stared. "Let's take these two boxes back to HALL, Kate. We've got to open them right now. They may have valuable clues inside them."

Kate cut loose the unused part of her ball of string and shoved it into her pocket. Then she stooped, lifted the box, cradled it in her cast, and together they went back up the stony slippery path to the place where they had found the first box. Oscar leaned down and picked it up, and they returned to the big HALL.

"Let's open them right now," Kate said shaking hers.

"Can't. We left the hatchet in the pines," Oscar said.

"Then we'll open them when we go up for lunch."

"They're probably empty," Oscar said warning her against disappointment. Kate shook hers again, but there was no sound or movement inside. They sank back looking at each other. "Why? Why? Why?" Oscar mused. "Why three empty boxes in three different places around HALL? It couldn't have just happened. Someone had to put them here."

"But who?"

"Beats me." Oscar leaned over and ran his hand over the outside of each box. "Empty inside, but . . ."

"It's crazy . . . empty boxes all around HALL. Someone had to put them there. And that someone probably had a very good reason."

"But why?" Oscar asked again. "Why would anyone put fake boxes all around HALL? It gets crazier and crazier, doesn't it? But one thing we do know and that is that there's something mighty funny going on. People in their right minds don't put locked empty boxes all over the place."

"Oscar," Kate said, her face lighting up with her idea. "Crazy things . . . crazy *people*. Maybe the people who put these boxes here were crazy?"

"Hey," Oscar said. "Yeah . . . maybe. Were any of the Strawbridge family strange?"

"Don't ask me, but Mom'll know. She's lived here ever since she was a little girl when Grandma and Grandpa were alive."

"We've got to find out if there was a loony Strawbridge." Oscar crossed his eyes, scattered his hair across his forehead, pulled at his lips with his finger and burbled like an idiot. "Think crazy . . ."

"Think crazy and solve the Strawbridge Secret," Kate interrupted. Oscar laughed as he looked at his watch.

"We can ask your mom after we open the boxes." They leaped up, snuffed out the candles and left HALL, dragging the two boxes in the bag. They were so excited and in such a hurry that they left the door in the panel wide open. They clambered out the opening without even stopping to listen for hobos. The hot heat of noon hit them as they seized ROSE and went pell-mell up WATER BUG. They left their things in a jumble under the bush, and Oscar swung away on his crutches toward their place in the pines. Kate skipped after him, the bag over her shoulder.

This time, Kate didn't interfere as Oscar chipped each lock loose. A wild hope stirred in her as the first lid came open, but the box was empty. The second was empty also. They looked at each other.

"At least it's consistent," Oscar said trying to hide his disappointment. "Whoever put these around HALL did it for a reason, but it wasn't to hide anything, that's for sure. Come on, Kate, let's go talk to your mom. Hope she knows something that'll shed some light on all this." They got up and went to the house.

Mom was standing at the stove, stirring soup and reading a book. "Mom, can Oscar stay for lunch?" Kate yelled, banging on the hooked screen door. Mom almost dropped her book into the soup.

"Don't do that. You'll scare the baby out of a day's growth," she said shakily. She opened the screen. "Marvelous to see you, Oscar. You look fine. How's that ankle? I've been so worried about you," she said all in a rush.

"Fine, Mrs. Cummings. I can walk on it . . . see?" He walked around the table without his crutches.

"I'm so relieved," Mom beamed. "You gave us quite a scare that day." She took a deep breath and asked, "And how's your mother?"

"Fine. She's been away, but she's coming back tomorrow."

"How does she find Ashtabula after all these years?"

Oscar shrugged. "OK, I guess." Kate saw his hands opening and closing impatiently. "Mrs. Cummings . . ." he began, but she interrupted him again.

"And how's your grandfather?" Adults, Kate fumed.

"Fine. But . . . ah . . . Mrs. Cummings . . . may I ask you something?"

"Of course, Oscar."

"Were any of the Strawbridges loony?" Mom almost burst out laughing, but Oscar's tense face made her choke it back.

"Why, Oscar, what a question."

"It's terribly important, Mrs. Cummings, and we thought you might know because you're so old . . ."

"Not *that* old," Mom smiled, putting her book on top of the oven. "The last Strawbridge died in 1894. I didn't know them, but my father did. He bought the place from them a year before they died, and he'd been farming it for seven years before that for the twins."

"But did he ever say any of the Strawbridges were loony?"

"Well," Mom said, a nostalgic look coming into her eyes. "It's odd that you should ask that, Oscar. There was talk about all the Strawbridges. Awfully standoffish family . . . no friends in the community . . . but good people, you understand . . . just strange. But the last of the Strawbridges were the strangest. They were twin girls who lived to just what age no one ever knew. And do you know what they did? They gradually sold off everything on the place: furniture, wagons, farm equipment, dishes, even family pictures. And the day they died nothing was left on this huge old farm except their double bed, a sampler over their bed, and a marble-topped chest of drawers. Those two died the same day in the same bed in this huge empty house. Would you call that loony?" She smiled down at them. Oscar and Kate stood openmouthed.

"How come they did that?" Oscar asked.

"Nobody knows," Mom said.

"How come your father bought it?"

"That's strange too. There weren't any Straw-bridges to leave it to. There were nine children in all . . . seven boys and these twin girls. They were years younger than the boys . . . an afterthought, the town always said. From that big family there wasn't one descendant . . . not one . . ."

"So your father bought it?"

"Yes. Dad was a good farmer. He worked most of it off and paid the rest in gold."

"When was that?"

"1894."

"What happened to the gold he paid for the farm?" Mom shook her head, puzzled.

"You know, Oscar, I don't know. I never gave it

much thought, but there must have been quite an estate . . ." Mom put her chin in her hands and started to drift off into her dream world, but Kate intercepted her.

"So Grandpa was the first owner after the Strawbridges?"

"Yes."

"Did he ever ask about the Secret?" Oscar pushed forward.

"Dad didn't believe in the legend, and he wouldn't tolerate gossip about the twins. He said they were two of the finest women he'd ever known; they'd treated him fair and square, and that was that."

"What kind of gossip?" Kate asked.

"Set the table, honey." Mom changed the subject abruptly.

"But what kind of gossip, Mrs. Cummings?" Oscar persisted.

"Enough," Mom said with finality. She went to the door and called lunch. Josh and Simone and Margaret came dragging in, dusty and hot. They washed in the sink. "How far did you get in the weeding?" Mom asked.

"We did half a row of beets," Margaret piped up.

"That's all?" Mom's face fell.

"It's hot out there," Josh complained.

"Yeah, hot out there." Simone mimicked him perfectly.

Kate sipped her soup, but she didn't taste it. Stupid trivial conversation when there were secrets to be solved. She and Oscar . . . they might be on the brink . . . the very brink of a breakthrough, if only they could get Mom alone again and in the right mood.

A knock at the screen door startled them. Kate looked up, frightened.

A hobo stood there cap in hand.

Make him go away, Mom, Kate prayed. This day was too important to be spoiled by hobos.

# *Chapter 10*

Mom rose and approached the hooked screen door eyeing the man carefully.

"I'd be glad to work the afternoon for you, missus, for a bite to eat." Kate twisted her hands in her lap. "I'm real handy," the hobo pleaded.

"You're from Brooklyn, aren't you?" Mom asked, her hand on the hook.

"How'd you guess?" He crushed his cap in his bony hands.

"Your accent." Mom opened the screen, and he stepped shyly into the kitchen. Ten eyes stared up at him from the table, even Kate's. "Haven't heard it since I was in college in New York . . . and how I do miss it. Josh, bring that stool for the man. Here's soup and crackers and salad." She grabbed dishes from the table and set them on the drainboard before him. He stuffed his cap into his pocket, moved to the sink to wash his grimy hands, sat down and picked up his spoon. The first bite was slow and dignified, but as the rich vegetable and beef soup went down, he suddenly lowered his head and began shoveling it into his mouth in great, gulping, burning mouthfuls. Crackers disappeared into his mouth whole.

"Children," Mom said very low. Their eyes swung about, all except Josh's.

"Joshua," Mom said. He half turned around. "Finish your lunch," Mom said evenly. She didn't look at the hobo again and began talking about the afternoon. "Josh, you've got to move on those weeds. Do two rows and then come in, and I'll have peanut butter cookies and lemonade for you. And if you get five rows done, maybe we can have a picnic at the lake tonight to cool off."

"Ya-hoooooo!" Josh let out a war whoop that made the hobo choke. Simone and Oscar looked at each other. Mom saw the look.

"Would you like to come to the lake with us?"

"Could we?" Simone almost jumped out of her chair.

"Of course . . . that is . . . if your grandfather approves."

"I'll make him." Simone rubbed her sunburned nose and turned to stare at the hobo again. He saw the stare and smiled.

"Name's Michael Lord. What's yours?"

"Simone Evangeline Witherspoon."

"Pretty name." Mr. Lord picked up his soup bowl and drank the last drops. He stuffed more crackers into his mouth. "Mrs. Witherspoon, I do thank you . . ."

"She's not my mother," Simone burst out.

"I'm Mrs. Cummings," Mom explained. "Simone and Oscar are neighbor children, and these are three of my four: Margaret, Kate and Joshua."

"Pleased to meet you, I'm sure." He tweaked one of Margaret's golden curls. "Me and my missus wanted a little girl, but we got three boys, boom, boom, boom." He looked longingly at the children, at the table with its bright blue tablecloth and the bowl of fresh fruit in the middle, the soup kettle simmering on the stove and the perking coffeepot. He wiped his hand across his eyes.

"How old are your boys?" Mom asked in her softest, kindest voice.

"When I left, they was two, four and seven; but it's been eight months. . . ." Desperately he went on. "You see, lost my job first thing when the hard times hit. Heard there was work in Texas, went there, but there wasn't none after all, so I'm just riding the rods, lookin', lookin' . . ." His voice trailed off.

"Well, you can be of service here this afternoon," Mom said briskly. "The garden's full of weeds, and if you could help Josh. . . . Seems like things have piled up something awful this last month since it's been so hot. . . ." She heaved herself from her chair and poured coffee for him.

"When's the baby due?" he asked very politely.

"Any day now," Mom laughed and fanned with her apron. "The sooner the better. This heat just doesn't agree with me."

"At least it's warm sleeping nights," Mr. Lord mumbled.

"Oh." Mom caught her breath.

"What's it like riding the rods?" Josh demanded.

"Josh," Mom said severely.

"That's OK, Mrs. Cummings." Mr. Lord slapped Josh manlike on the back. "Come on, squirt. Show me that garden, and I'll tell you a tale or two while we make those old weeds wish they'd never been born." Oscar hobbled up and after them. Kate stood with her hands on her hips, glaring after the traitor.

"You go with them, Kate," Mom said. "I'll clear away." Kate looked back at Mom. Did she dare bring up the Strawbridge twins? . . . But Mom was already picking up her book, and Kate knew it was too late. She went to the garden and plunked herself down beside Oscar.

"Fine secret-solver you are," she sneered.

"Shut up," Oscar said rudely. He dug at the crab grass that was choking the new bean sprouts. Kate wanted to hit him.

Mr. Lord was digging so fast that the aisles were

filled with weeds. Josh and Simone worked in the rows on either side of him, weeding at top speed. "Being a hobo ain't no picnic. You learn mighty fast which towns have strict police and which ones easy. And the bulls—you know, them detectives the railroads hire to run us bums off the freights—they can either wink at you or club you. All depends. But you get clued-in quick. Hobos stick together. Most help each other, share what little food they have. Everyone's in the same fix, after all . . ."

"But hobos fight," Josh shouted. "I saw three fight over a chicken . . ."

"Sure," Mr. Lord said. "There's always a few rotten apples in a barrel, but mostly we pull together. Knowed a man, big strapping fellow, had a slice of bread, only one measly slice, and he divided it like it was a kingdom and gave me half."

All afternoon Mr. Lord held them spellbound. At four, Mom brought out a jug of lemonade and some freshly baked cookies, and they sprawled in the shade of the oak eating and resting and talking. When they finished, Mr. Lord rose. "Got to be shoving on," he said.

"I have something in the kitchen for you," Mom said. At the house she gave him a brown paper bag tied with a string.

"Thank you, thank you." He bowed humbly, but there was a manly tilt to his shoulders. "Missus, you don't know what you've done for me."

"I just wish I could have done more." Mom smiled.

"Well . . ." Mr. Lord stood hat in hand.

"What?"

"Could I beg a piece of paper and a stamp? I haven't written to the missus for a long time now." Mom got the paper, an envelope and a stamp and a pencil. She put them on the table, and Mr. Lord sat down. The children clustered around him like bees.

"Shoo." Mom waved her arms at the ring. "Give the man a minute's peace." She stepped outside and said, "Show me what you did in the garden." They escorted her like a queen, and she exclaimed with wonder at their industry . . . and Mr. Lord's. Half the garden was done.

"Let's go see if he's finished," Josh yelled and led the way back to the kitchen, but Mr. Lord was gone. On the table was a paper napkin on which was written, "God bless you, Mrs. Cummings."

"Wait, Mr. L!" Josh and Simone rushed to the front of the house. But the hobo had vanished with his sack and his letter. They ran all the way to the railroad tracks, but soon they returned disgruntled and sweaty. Kate knew why they were so angry. They had been begging Mr. Lord to take them with him. They flopped down on the lawn and chewed on grass stems. Just then Margaret came racing up.

"Come quick. Look what I found." They jumped

up, and Kate and Oscar followed. "There." Margaret pointed.

On the second picket of the fence amid the lilac bushes were two strange marks. The one on top was faint, but the one below looked new and bold. They looked like this.

"What are they?" Josh asked. They rushed into the house and dragged Mom to the fence.

"Oh." She put her hand over her mouth. "Don't know for sure, but I have my suspicions. We'll ask your father when he comes."

"But what do you think?" Simone persisted, unable to wait.

"Well," Mom said. "I've heard that hobos have a code, and they mark houses with signs." Kate and Oscar exchanged a glance.

"What kind of signs—and why?" Josh asked.

"Well, like a sign that would mean in this house there was a 'kind woman' or 'noisy dog' or 'meal if you work for it' or 'well guarded' . . . all things that hobos need to know. But I never saw any of the signs before. And this looks like two, doesn't it?"

"One's faint, and the other's bright," Simone said.

"Chalk or crayon . . ." Mom rubbed it gingerly. "We'll have to wait till your father comes, he'll know for sure."

Dad and Nathan came exactly at five-fifteen. The children showed them the chalked fence picket. "Hobo signs," Dad said at once. He leaned closer. "Don't know exactly what they mean, but this one probably means man or woman. See the figure? See, stars in her crown." He laughed. "But this." He looked at it carefully. "I don't understand this. That's new . . . wait a minute. You say your hobo worked this afternoon? Well, he's the first hobo that's done that. We've given lots of food out, but this is the first one to work. So that could mean work for a meal. Don't know, but I'd guess Mr. Lord put it there fresh this afternoon when he left."

"He was a nice man, even if he was a hobo," Kate said. Dad put his hand on her neck and pulled her against him.

"Hobos could be me or Mr. Morgan . . ." He looked over their heads at Mom. Mom blew him a kiss to keep from crying.

Simone raced home for permission to go to the lake and came back in her suit. She caught up with Josh and Margaret who were showing Dad the partially weeded garden. Mom sang in the kitchen where Kate and Oscar helped wrap sandwiches. Everyone got into his suit and piled into the car, and Dad drove to the lake.

Oscar and Kate sat against the big log and whispered. "You've got to find out from your mom about those twins. There's something she's not telling us," Oscar said. Kate nodded. It was up to her. Oscar had tried and had been rebuffed. She had to do it.

But how?

# Chapter 11

The rattle of glass woke Kate. The milkman hurried up the front walk swinging his wire carrier, whistling. Mr. Frizzell plunked the bottles into the box on the front step, then ran back to the waiting truck, empty bottles tinkling. He gunned the motor and turned away toward the mansion on the hill.

Kate snapped to a sitting position. She had to talk to Mom about the twins . . . right now. "I'll start the coffee," she whispered to Mom when they met in the hall. Mom blew her a sleepy kiss as she went in to wake Nathan.

Kate unhooked the front screen and lifted one quart of milk from the box and pressed it into her stomach with her cast. Plans swirled in her head as she stored the milk in the refrigerator and began to make the coffee. How could she get Mom to talk today when she wouldn't yesterday? Should she sidle into the subject, hint at it, pretend indifference, be honest?

Mom's soft step came down the stairs. She went straight to the stove, poured the half-done coffee into a white cup and took an eager sip. She shook her head, sighed, and took another long sip. She didn't look ready for the twins yet, so Kate ran to get another quart of milk. She put it in the refrigerator and ran to get another. By the last trip she had made up her mind. She rushed to the kitchen. "Mom, why? . . ." Her foot caught in the doorsill between the dining room and the kitchen, and the milk bottle slipped from under her cast and crashed to the floor.

Mom leaned against the stove, her hand across her eyes. Slowly she turned to look. "Kate, why can't you be more *careful?*" Tears smarted Kate's eyes.

"I was just trying to help." She knelt and began picking up jagged pieces of bottle.

"Get away. You'll cut yourself next." Kate hovered helplessly while Mom cleaned up.

Dad clattered down the back stairs. Trembling, Mom turned to get breakfast. Kate felt as if someone had pulled the plug and her life had drained out of her. She slumped into her chair and put her chin in her hand so that Dad couldn't see her stricken face.

But Dad didn't sit down. "Hurry up, Nathan," he yelled up the stairs. He grabbed his cap. "Forgot to tell you, honey, but Old Man Porch is sending the limousine down for a tune-up this morning, and I've got to have it ready to go by ten 'cause Mrs. Witherspoon's coming home from somewhere or other. Think, honey, real money . . . cash." He kissed her exuberantly, then rushed to the garage. Mom took two lunches from the refrigerator and gave them to the trailing Nathan. They watched the car chug out the drive behind the lilac bushes.

Kate glanced at the clock. Mrs. Witherspoon . . . on the noon train. She *had* to ask Mom even though she was mad. "Mom, why won't you tell me about the Strawbridge twins?"

"I have my reasons."

"But what reasons?" Kate came over and stood close to her and put a hand on her shoulder. "Mom, I have to know. It's important . . . the most important thing in my life."

"The most important thing in your life," Mom repeated meaninglessly.

"And Oscar's life too." Kate gulped, looked to heaven, then rushed ahead heedlessly. "It's about the Secret. Oscar and I . . . we've almost solved the Secret."

Mom jerked back in surprise, but Kate didn't stop. "Down WATER BUG we found HALL, see, filled with empty boxes, but someone had to put them there, and we think it was those loony twins, if they were loony, and you won't tell us," she finished breathlessly. Mom was instantly awake.

"WATER BUGS, Oscar, empty? . . ." she repeated in bewilderment.

"Mom, listen." Kate began speaking as if to a child. "I found HALL, that's a code name for this cave, see? I found the first box, and then we found the second and third, and it has lots of tunnels, but we have string so we won't get lost like Tom and Becky, so you don't have to worry, and that's why I need more batteries. Please, Mom, did the loony twins put these boxes there? Someone had to."

"Now let me get this straight." Mom sat up very purposefully. "You and Oscar found a cave with water bugs in it . . ."

"WATER BUG is code for riverbank."

"So you and Oscar have found a cave in the riverbank. And you've been exploring it and have found some empty boxes. Right?"

"Right."

"So you two have been up to things behind my back?"

"No, no." Kate's whole body quivered. "We aren't doing it behind *your* back, only Josh's and Simone's and Margaret's. We're Cripples Incorporated, Oscar and me, because they won't play with us. Oscar made me promise not to tell a soul about HALL, but now I've told you, but you see how important it is, really, really important. You may have the crucial clue."

But Mom wasn't thinking about clues. A worried look spread over her face. "This cave . . . you say you and Oscar have been in it already? How many times?"

Kate drew back. Mom's voice had an ominous tone in it. "Only three . . ."

"And how far have you explored? How far back into the hill?" Kate's heart sank. Oscar had been right; she shouldn't have told a soul.

"Pretty far," she faltered truthfully. Mom grabbed her shoulders.

"You and Oscar are *never, never* to enter that cave again!" Her fingers dug into Kate's soft skin. "It-is-very-dangerous. You-could-suffocate-get-lost-fall-in-to-a-crevice-or-" She grimaced in horror. "Promise-me-this-instant-that-you-will-never-go-in-there-again."

"But, Mom . . ."

"*Promise me this instant!*" She shook Kate hard.

"I'll promise if . . ."

"No ifs . . . promise!" Mom rattled her head with a frantic shake.

"Only one tiny if," Kate cried desperately. "You promise not to tell . . . not even Dad about HALL and WATER BUG. If Oscar and I can't solve the Secret, he won't come here anymore, and it's all we've got, now that we're both *cripples*."

"Cripples . . ." Mom repeated tonelessly her eyes on Kate's cast. Perspiration beaded her face and neck.

Kate waited helplessly. She waited and waited, then finally she got up and went to the screen. "Honey," Mom's voice had lost its tension. "I don't mean to scold, but you're just too young to think about all the things that could happen to you. You and Oscar have had enough trouble this summer to last you both a month of Sundays. It's a wonder you're still . . ." She stopped.

"Alive," Kate filled in silently for her.

"You and Oscar play here in the yard where I can keep an eye on you. Look for the Secret here. You can still have plenty of fun and mystery and all that right here in the house," she assured her, trying to lift the gloom from Kate's face.

"Sure, sure," Kate said with false cheerfulness. "Right here under everyone's nose." Mom smiled her old smile.

"I won't tell a soul, I promise." Kate unhooked the screen. "Where to?" Mom asked, the worried look returning to her face.

"Just to the pines," Kate answered. She found herself in her secret place but couldn't remember how she'd gotten there. Blabbermouth! How could she face Oscar? What could she say?

He came bursting in. "What'd she say?" he demanded. Kate couldn't look at him. "Spill it," he said kneeling eagerly before her.

Kate slowly lifted her eyelashes. "Oscar," she

faltered, "I did something awful."

"What?"

"I told Mom about HALL, and she got furious and said we can't go there anymore . . . ever." She recounted the whole terrible scene. After she had finished, they sat there avoiding each other's eyes. Oscar sifted pine needles through his fingers and gnawed on his lip. "We could look in the room where the twins died," Kate said after a long time. Oscar lifted his head.

"Better doing that than sitting here like two corpses," he said. "Only thing is, we might run into Simone or Josh or someone."

"We'll think of something to tell them." Kate sprang up. But Oscar didn't move.

"Think of a good reason to be in the room, then we'll go."

"We can say we're looking for Blackie."

"That's good enough." They went into the house. They encountered no one and went up the front stairs as quietly as they could. The door to the guest room was always kept closed so it would stay cleaner. Kate opened it softly, and they slipped in.

# Chapter 12

The bed was a big four-poster covered with white muslin. A lavender and white quilt covered the bed. A marble-topped dresser stood by the window, and a sampler motto hung on the wall by the bed. Ruffled muslin curtains hung at the windows, and the wall-paper was lavender forget-me-nots. The wide floor-boards were waxed and bare. Oscar went to the bed and ran his hand up and down the post. Kate did the same with another post. They felt, rubbed, pressed, smoothed, poked and fingered the wooden parts of the bed. They tore off the bedding and lifted the mattress.

Nothing.

They turned to the dresser. Stealthily they pulled out every drawer, looked in every nitch, behind, under and on top.

Nothing.

They remade the bed and sat down on the edge of it. Oscar's eyes looked up and down the room.

The sampler motto. He reached up and lifted it from its hook. At the top, outlined in rust yarn, was an oddly shaped building; long and narrow and low with a slanting roof at the end. Below were seven short lines done in black chain stitch.

THE LIBERTY WELL

MEASURE FOR MEASURE
ROUND STEPS, THEN THE LABYRINTH
TRUTH AND FREEDOM
HIDDEN FROM FALSE MEN
EMPTY IT SEEMS
BUT THEREIN LIES THE TALE

Kate read it over his shoulder. "Funny," she giggled. "I've dusted that a hundred times and never read it before."

"It doesn't make sense," Oscar said.

"Doesn't even rhyme," Kate scorned. "It should rhyme like 'Home Sweet Home' or 'Welcome is our guest/May he truly rest' or . . ."

"LABYRINTH," Oscar mused. "Kate, you called HALL a labyrinth, remember?"

"Yeah, I remember."

"TRUTH AND FREEDOM. Slaves, freedom, labyrinth, cave . . ." his voice trailed off.

"Oh, Oscar," Kate said. "Could it be a code like TOAD HALL and WATER BUG?"

"It just might be." Oscar shook the sampler. "It just could be. Oh, Kate, Kate, it just could be!" They looked at each other in awe. "Get some paper so we can copy this."

Kate ran to her desk and got a yellow tablet and a pencil. Oscar's hand trembled as he copied the words and drew in the funny building at the top and all the squiggly lines framing it. They sneaked out of the house and back to their secret place in the pines without encountering Margaret or Josh or Simone.

"Mom's coming on the noon train." Oscar looked at his watch. "I won't be able to come here anymore, but we can't stop now. We're onto something for sure, I can feel it in my bones."

"Me, too."

"But if I can't come, how in Hades are we going to work on this?"

"We can leave notes for each other here."

"But I couldn't come to get them," Oscar said.

"The telephone?"

"Someone would hear." They lapsed into a discouraged silence. The precious minutes ticked away.

"I know," Kate burst out. "Our code—with the numbers instead of the letters. We'll send letters in our code." Oscar's face brightened.

"Hey, why didn't I think of that." He hit himself on the head as if to jar his brain loose. Their relief was so great that their coming separation no longer

THE LIBERTY WELL
MEASURE FOR MEASURE
ROUND STEPS, THEN THE LABYRINTH
TRUTH AND FREEDOM
HIDDEN FROM FALSE MEN
EMPTY IT SEEMS
BUT THEREIN LIES THE TALE

seemed so final. They returned to the mysterious motto.

"MEASURE FOR MEASURE . . . length, ruler, yardstick . . ." Oscar said.

"Measure like in music . . . notes between two bars on the musical staff . . ." Kate suggested. "Or in cooking. Mom has little measuring cups."

"Music, for music, music for cups, measuring music, music, ruler, yardstick, music . . ." Oscar shifted the words around and around. Nothing made sense.

"Try the next line."

"ROUND STEPS, THEN THE LABYRINTH."

"Whoever saw round steps?"

"I did once leading up to a monument. The steps curved like this." Oscar made an arc with his arm.

"No monuments around here," Kate said.

"Let's try another way," Oscar said. "Let's skip every other word. MEASURE—MEASURE—STEPS—THE—TRUTH—FREEDOM—FROM—MEN—IT—BUT—LIES—TALE. That's no good. FOR—ROUND—THEN—LABYRINTH—AND—HIDDEN—FALSE—EMPTY—SEEMS—THEREIN—THE—"

"Every third word," Kate suggested. They tried it every way and nothing worked.

"Backwards," Oscar said. But that didn't make sense either. Kate leaned back, but Oscar kept on doggedly. He knew lots of different ways to manipulate the words and letters, but nothing was right. It got closer and closer to noon.

"Oscar, what are we going to do?" Kate wailed.

"Don't be a nincompoop," he said calmly. "Just think what we do know. The LABYRINTH is HALL, and FREEDOM has to do with the slaves, so that makes this the clue we've been looking for. The Secret's right here in these words, Kate. We just have to figure out what those twins meant."

"But I can't wait!" she exclaimed.

"You'll have to," Oscar said practically. "Even Sherlock Holmes didn't solve his mysteries in a minute. It always takes a whole story or book. I've read lots of mysteries, but Sherlock Holmes is the best. You ever read him?" Kate shook her head. "He's great. That's where I got the idea for every second word or every third word. He's always fooling around with cryptograms."

"Crip-toe-what?"

"Cryptograms," Oscar repeated. "You know, secret writing . . . codes." A train whistle came faintly through the pines. "Mom." Oscar leaped up and seized his crutches. "See you around."

"Write," Kate called after him. She watched the pine limbs slowly come to rest again, and she felt as if the sun had gone under a thundercloud. But she had enough spirit left to spell out the name of the crip-toe-game man . . . Sureluck Homes.

She listened to the train rumble onto the trestle. Go back, Mrs. Witherspoon, go back. She shook her fist at the trestle. But the train came on, slowed and stopped at the station, and Kate knew that the great gray limousine was waiting. She got up and went into the house. There she went straight to the guest room and copied the motto and worked on it until lunch. She got very discouraged. She didn't have Oscar's sense for such tedious work. At lunch she asked, "Mom, may I go to the library?"

"Of course." Kate ate quickly, then got *Little Women* and walked into town, looking at herself in the dusty windows of the empty stores as she went down Main Street. The library was on a side street, and she mounted the steps, returned her book and looked in the children's room for Sureluck Homes. She looked on the shelf under H, then S. He wasn't there. Finally, frustrated, she asked Mrs. Dynamite at the desk.

"Oh, that's in the adult department," she said. "It's not a book for little girls."

"But I have to have it." Kate stood on tiptoes. But Mrs. Dynamite turned away and began counting the fine money. Kate drifted home without the book. She drooped around all afternoon unable to concentrate on the motto or anything else. How she missed Oscar!

"Thinking about your cave?" Mom asked coming on her sprawled listlessly on the side porch.

"No," Kate said. "Mrs. Dynamite wouldn't let me take out Sureluck Homes because I'm not adult enough." Mom laughed.

"Why didn't you tell me that's what you wanted, honey. I have Sherlock. Bought it at a little second-hand bookstore near campus when I was in college in New York. It's up in the bookcase in my bedroom."

The sun returned to Kate's day, and she raced upstairs. There she found Sureluck Homes . . . Sherlock Holmes . . . in two worn volumes. She seized them, crossed the hall and flopped down on her bed, where she read until she fell asleep.

That evening they went to the lake; the only relief from the stifling heat. Kate sat perspiring against the log, watching the family in the water. Mom's hat and book were the only calm things in sight. Everyone was splashing and yelling, but Kate didn't envy them. She propped the yellow tablet on her knees, wet the tip of her pencil with her tongue and wrote:

26922 2126 412916181320 1213 14127712? 18 2614
9222623181320 8. 19121514228. 1922 188 1926923.
242613 2126 813222616 264262? 19127, 19619?
141214 188 14614 26251267 19261515 812 21269.
14'1526232

Finished she folded it slowly and stuffed it into an envelope. It already had a stamp on it, and it was addressed to:

Mr. Oscar Witherspoon
The Mansion on Bank Street
Ashtabula, Ohio

She hid it among the sheets of the tablet and felt immensely better. Later, after they got home, Kate sneaked across the street and slipped the letter into the big rural mailbox and put the red flag up. Mr. Pumper would get it in the morning.

Saturday was work day. Dad backed the Model A from the garage, and Josh began to sweep the floor while Nathan started cleaning and oiling the tools hanging in neat rows above the workbench. Kate hung about watching. The sun was fierce, and Dad opened the doors next to the garage and drove the car into the space where the Strawbridge carriage had once been kept, years ago. The car was too long, and Dad couldn't close the doors. "That's funny," he muttered. "It fits in the garage."

Kate thought about the motto. Did it say anything about room sizes?

"Oh, well." Dad shrugged and went to get the lawn mower.

Mom was doing the laundry. Josh and Nathan carried the heavy baskets of wet clothes from the cellar so they could be hung on the outdoors clothesline. Kate's job was to hang. She tolerated Margaret's "helping," her mind on the motto. After lunch Kate slipped out to the mailbox. Her letter was gone.

That evening they went to the lake again, and Kate wrote her second letter to Oscar.

9222623 7412 8. 19. 871298228. 418819 1922
241261523 19221511 68. 1922'23 14261622 141214
15227 68 223111512922 19261515. 19127, 19127,
19127. 419267 26922 2126 2312181320? 18'14
412916181320 1213 14127712 261323 202277181320
131241922922. 4918722.

14'1526232

She hid it in her room, ready for mailing on Monday.

Sunday was hot and still. The minister talked in long limp sentences. Margaret lay on the cushioned seat, her head in Dad's lap. He caressed her forehead with his thick, grease-stained fingers. Mom sat stiff and proper in her blue hat, but her eyes wandered up and down the sparsely filled pews and out the open window. Josh and Nathan slumped between Mom and Dad, sulky and itchy in their suits. Kate leaned her head over the back of the pew and looked at the ushers upside down.

At last the sermon ended, they wavered through the last hymn, the minister prayed over them for the final time. Then he walked to the rear door and stood, his neck bulging untidily over his collar, greeting the congregation as they straggled out into the stifling Sunday noon.

The day dragged. In the late afternoon they went for a drive, but it didn't cool them much. They couldn't go to the lake because it wasn't a proper thing to do on the Lord's Day. Kate worked on the motto until she drove herself crazy, then retreated into the world of Sherlock Holmes. Finally the day wasted itself away.

# Chapter 13

Monday, Kate sat at the base of the huge maple tree in the front yard watching for the mailman. Blackie, bloated with her babies, sat beside her. As Mr. Pumper drove up to the mailbox, Kate teetered on the edge of the road waiting to dash. "Got something for you, Kate." Mr. Pumper held the fistful of letters out the window. Without looking either way, Kate dashed into the road and slid to a stop by Mr. Pumper's dusty old car.

"Thanks, Mr. P.," she said seizing the envelopes. He waved, and the old car chugged on up the hill. Kate spread the mail on the grass before Blackie.

Mistress Katherine Cummings
The Strawbridge Place on Bank Street
Ashtabula, Ohio

She snatched it up and ripped it open, but the maze

of numbers made no sense. She needed the key. She shoved the letter into her waistband under Nathan's shirt and ran into the house.

Mom was sitting limply on a kitchen chair. Kate plopped the mail before her. "Thanks, honey." She didn't move to look at it as she usually did. "I just can't seem to get going this morning." She sighed, picking up her coffee cup and taking a long sip.

"You want me to do anything now?" Kate asked.

"Just keep an eye on Margaret for me, honey. She and Josh had a scrap, and she's all upset. Maybe you can calm her down with a book or something." The letter itched against Kate's skin.

A familiar whistle sent her racing to the side door. Mr. Gunn's bakery truck stood in the drive. Mom followed slowly, her feet apart, fanning with the pack of letters. Mr. Gunn doffed his cap. "Morning, Mrs. Cummings. Hot enough for you?"

"Oh my, oh my . . ." Mom fanned frantically.

"Hi there, Kate," he said as he opened the two doors on the back of the truck and pulled out all the drawers. Kate moved closer and breathed in the wonderful odors of chocolate and lemon and warm bread. "What'll it be today, Mrs. Cummings?"

But Mom's mind wasn't on food. "Just don't understand it. Never had a heat spell last this long that I can remember in all my years living on the lake."

"Gotta end sometime. If you ask me we're heading

for a whopper of a thunderstorm."

"I just wish it would come this minute." Mom sighed again. "I'm useless. Can't get anything baked and laid aside for Mr. Elmer and the children if and when I go to the hospital . . . it's just awful. So, guess I'd better get some provisions from you. Pecan roll this morning?"

Kate shivered with delight. Pecan rolls were usually saved for Sunday morning breakfast.

"Sure thing." Mr. Gunn pulled the third drawer all the way out with a flourish and selected the gooiest, most nut-encrusted roll and handed it to Kate.

Just then Josh charged around the house from one direction, Margaret from the other. Mr. Gunn caught Margaret and lifted her up so she could see and sniff. Josh stuck his nose into a towering coconut cream pie. "Can I go with you, Mr. Gunn?" Josh pleaded. "Please, Mr. Gunn, you said I could sometime, remember?"

"Hush, Josh. Don't bother the man," Mom said.

"That's OK, Mrs. Cummings. Could use an extra hand today."

"Yipeeeeeeeeee!" Josh shouted jumping into the cab. He seized the steering wheel and made sounds like a series of backfires.

"You're welcome to him." Mom smiled helplessly.

"He'll keep my mind off the heat." Mr. Gunn

winked and wiped his neck with his big blue bandana.

"Have an apple pie?"

"Fresh this morning." Mr. Gunn pulled open the top drawer.

"And three loaves of bread, two brown, one white." Mom counted the coins twice from her worn change purse before she put the money into Mr. Gunn's hand. As they drove out of the drive, Josh leaned out and gave them a pitying look. They waved at him, then stored the sweets in the pantry. Mom collapsed at the table again and picked up her coffee cup.

Kate and Margaret retreated quietly. Kate read to her for awhile, then Margaret began playing with her paper dolls. Kate tiptoed up to her room and closed the door. She took the letter quickly from its hiding place and opened it.

1814 1216. 19124 26922 2126? 18'14 9222623181320 151278 26251267 71922 613232292091261323 92618159122623 261323 21222215 19261515 261323 14127712 26922 141287 181411129726137 24156228 812 21269. 2614 9222623181320 81922915122416 19121514228. 1926522 2126 22311151292223 261321412922?

14'1512923

She got out the key she'd made and figured out the message. Then she kissed the letter, folded it into a tiny square and hid it in her dresser. She flopped down on the bed thinking about the motto, Oscar's letter, the Secret. Too excited to lie still, she leaped up and raced up the attic stairs to search, but the stifling air drove her back downstairs and she raced to the cellar and began poking in the coal bin. By lunch time she'd searched the furnace room, behind all the glass jars in Mom's canning cupboard and in the laundry room.

"Where in the world?" Mom demanded. Kate went close to her and whispered.

"The Secret."

"A bath, young lady, this instant. And drop those filthy clothes in the washing machine. No more of that today. You're to stay clean." Kate scowled and pounded up the back stairs to the bathroom.

After lunch Kate swept up both volumes of Sherlock Holmes and began to read furiously. It made her feel closer to Oscar. Between stories she tried to figure out more of the motto, but it stymied her completely. Supper was cold baked beans and sliced tomatoes and half the apple pie for dessert. Mom left the table to lie down right in the middle of supper.

It was the middle of the night when something woke Kate. Mom and Dad's door was ajar, spilling light into the hall. Cautiously she peered into the crack of the door.

Mom sat on the edge of their bed, a suitcase on the floor beside her. She rocked back and forth holding her huge abdomen, crooning and moaning. As Kate pushed the door open, Mom looked up startled, then bit her lips to keep back any further sounds.

Dad came hurrying out of the big closet, fastening his belt. He grabbed the suitcase and put the other arm around Mom. "Easy does it, precious," he said. Mom winced.

"Hurry, Edgar. The pains are awfully close together."

"Here, carry this." Dad thrust the suitcase at Kate, picked Mom up and carried her down the stairs. Kate followed, numbly. Dad ran to the garage to get the car. Lightning flashed and thunder mumbled in the west. Mom looked eagerly toward the storm.

"Maybe that's the whopper," she said half to herself, then she turned to Kate. "You're my big girl, Kate, and you and Nathan are going to have to look after things until Daddy can call Mr. Elmer and tell him to get over here. Don't let anything 'just happen' to you, Kate. I'm depending on you. . . ." A pain seized her, and she grabbed the porch post and hung on until it passed. "Wake Nathan and close all the windows. Mr. Elmer'll be here just as soon as Daddy can call him on the phone. And Daddy should be home soon because this baby's coming fast. Mr. Elmer should be here in an hour or so." She tried to smile. "Remember when he came when Margaret was born? He'll stay with you and Josh and Margaret while Daddy and Nathan are at the shop."

Dad drove up in the car, and she got in and Kate handed her the suitcase. Lightning flashed, and the thunder rumbled close behind. "Daddy, your umbrella," Kate yelled.

"Forget it," Dad shouted. The engine coughed, then roared, and the car lurched down the driveway and turned into the road without stopping. A breeze lifted Kate's tangled hair as she stood staring after them. Lightning and thunder filled the western horizon.

Kate shuddered, hurried inside and locked the door. She flew up the stairs trying not to think that she was the only one awake in the creaky old house. She pounded on Nathan and shook him awake. "The baby's coming," she said as he rubbed his eyes.

Nathan seemed to know at once what had happened and got up and plodded about, pigeon-toed, closing windows. Kate stayed at his heels. The storm was coming fast like the baby.

Margaret woke up and began crying for Mommy. Kate was just going to her when Josh burst into the living room. "What's up?" he asked.

"Dad took Mom to the hospital," Nathan said. "And a storm's coming."

"Hope it's Mr. Gunn's whopper," Josh said. Both

boys watched the advancing storm as they went from window to window.

"I want Mommy," Margaret wailed from the stairs. Kate ran up and led her down into the living room.

"She's at the hospital having the baby," Kate soothed, but Margaret wouldn't be soothed. She cried and cried. The lightning and thunder increased, and the breeze became a wind. Margaret buried her head under the couch cushions and screamed. Nathan and Josh were in the den closing the last windows. The lightning flashed so rapidly now that it turned the night into day, and the thunder was continuous. The first great drops of rain splattered against the bay window. Nathan and Josh unhooked the front screen. Blasts of cool air poured through the house. Kate crept to the door, her fingers in her ears. Nathan stood on the edge of the porch getting sprayed by the fierce rain, and Josh teetered on the porch railing, hanging onto a post. Margaret's howls were lost in the turbulence.

The storm swept on relentlessly. The rain came down in sheets. Suddenly a vivid streak of lightning and an immediate crash of thunder roared around the porch. Nathan staggered back, and Josh fell from the railing. They dived through the doorway and slammed the door. The lights winked off, then on again. Nathan and Josh dripped on the floor. They all stared at each other. The wails from the couch got louder.

"Can't you shut her up?" Nathan jerked his head toward Margaret.

"You shut her up," Kate retorted. "She's your sister, too." Nathan didn't answer. He plodded toward the little bathroom off the den and soon returned with a dry towel draped about his hips. Josh did the same.

"We'd better get some candles, just in case," Nathan said. "Kate, you know where Mom keeps them?"

Kate headed for the sideboard, and Nathan sat down beside Margaret and cuddled her. Josh helped Kate stick candle stubs into holders, and then he ran to the kitchen for the match box on the oven. But before he could return, a blaze of lightning and a monster thunderclap put the lights out. He groped his way to the dining room, and somehow he and Kate got candles lighted with their shaking fingers. They hurried into the living room to be near Nathan, and they all sat silent and scared as the thunder boomed like artillery about the roof. Margaret sat in Nathan's lap, her fingers in her ears.

"When did Mom and Dad go?" Josh shouted over the thunder and wind.

"Just before I woke Nathan," Kate yelled back.

"Wonder if the baby's been born yet?"

"Do you want a boy or a girl?" Nathan asked.

"A boy," Josh said loudly. "It had better be a boy."

"It'd better be a girl," Kate said stoutly.

"Boy," Nathan said. "Dad told the guys at the shop he had a boy's name all picked out."

"What?"

"Joseph Nicholson." They thought about that for a minute.

"We'll call him Little Joe," Josh said.

The storm encircled the house. It rattled the windows, lifted a shutter from its mountings and slammed it against the house. The thunder never stopped, and the rain pelted down so solidly that they couldn't see the street.

"I'm hungry," Josh announced. They all trailed into the kitchen, and Josh and Nathan went into the pantry and came back with the apple pie. Josh opened the refrigerator to get a bottle of milk. "Fridge is broken." He looked up at the electric clock. It had stopped at 12:58. Margaret watched them devour the rest of the pie, but she wouldn't take her fingers from her ears to eat her piece. Josh ate it for her.

They finished the pecan roll and ate half a loaf of white bread with butter and brown sugar heaped on each slice. Nathan rubbed his stomach and stretched. "Wonder what time it is?" he said looking up at the stopped clock.

"When's Mr. Elmer coming?" Kate asked. "Mom said he'd be here soon as Dad called him."

"I'll call him." Nathan got up, and they all got up and followed him into the den, unable to be alone. But the phone was dead. They looked at each other. The dead phone gave Kate a hollow, uneasy feeling. How long they stood there, clustered together, Kate didn't know. Finally Margaret took her fingers from her ears and rubbed her eyes. Kate took her into the living room, and she crawled onto the couch. She fell asleep instantly. Josh and Nathan stood at the long front windows watching the rain spill over the gutters and cascade to the walk below. Huge puddles drowned the lawn.

"It's a cloudburst," Nathan said letting the curtain drop. He stretched again. "Come on, Josh, let's go to bed."

"What'll we do with Margaret?" Kate asked.

"Leave her here," Nathan said heading for the door.

"I don't want to sleep alone," Kate yelled, hesitating between Margaret and the door. "I'm sca . . ."

"Fraidy cat." Josh hopped up and down like a goblin. "Fraidy cat, fraidy ca . . ."

"Shut up, Josh." Nathan turned around very deliberately and looked from Kate to the sleeping Margaret. "Want to build a tent like we used to when we were little?"

"Yeah," Josh whooped. He rushed into the dining room and began dragging chairs into the living room and turning them on their sides. Nathan went to their bedroom and got the sheets from the beds. Kate and Josh helped drape the sheets over the chairs, and they made a cozy white flat-topped tent. Josh was the first to crawl in on his knees and elbows, carrying his candle, and almost losing his towel. Nathan followed with his candle, and Kate came last with her candle. They settled themselves and lay on the rug, warmed by each other's presence in the soft luminous whiteness.

"OK, Kate?" Nathan asked.

"Great." They exchanged a glance and smile that Josh didn't see.

The storm faded away to the east. Before long, they were all asleep, and the candles burned down silently and went out in a sputter of melted wax.

# Chapter 14

Kate woke stiff and chill, rubbed her eyes and looked about sleepily. Instantly she remembered last night. She crawled out of the tent and pushed the curtain back. She gasped. The puddles had become great pools of water, and it was still raining; not the big pelting drops of last night, but thin, slanty rain.

She went to the back door and opened it. No meowing cat sat there. The garage doors stood wide and empty, and the carriage doors were open too, blown askew by the wind. She glanced automatically up at the clock. It still said 12:58. She flicked the light switch.

Nothing.

She opened the refrigerator, and a warm sour smell assaulted her.

She woke Nathan, then dressed. The gas stove still worked, so she made coffee. The aroma from the perking pot made her feel more normal. She and Nathan sat at opposite ends of the table and ate sugar bread. "It's still raining," Kate said.

"Yeah," Nathan answered.

"Wonder where Dad is? Mom said last night that he'd be home in just a couple of hours because the baby was coming fast. And where's Mr. Elmer?"

"It's the storm's fault," Nathan said. He got up, took a cup and poured some coffee into it. He added sugar just the way Dad did, took a swallow, grimaced, then took another. Kate watched him.

Josh swooped in, his towel dangerously low on his hips. He looked from Nathan to Kate and back again. "Where's Dad?" Nathan shrugged, his mouth full. "That storm must have been the whopper that Mr. Gunn said was coming," Josh said looking out the window.

"Worst whopper I've ever seen." Nathan pushed his half-drunk coffee from him, wiped his lips with the back of his hand the way Dad did. He stood up. "Dad must be stranded somewhere or went straight to the shop from the hospital. I'd better get down to the shop."

"Can I go with you?" Josh asked eagerly. Nathan grinned thoughtfully.

"Guess I could use an extra hand in case Dad's not there." Josh leaped up the steep stairs and was back in a minute, dressed. They dragged on boots and raincoats, took Dad's umbrella and set out.

Kate stood by the door the way Mom did. She watched Josh jump in all the puddles as they crossed the yard. Leaves, twigs and some large branches lay twisted and black on the lawn. Kate shivered, closed the door and locked it. She leaned against it thinking. Was Mom all right? Was the baby born yet? Where was Dad? And Blackie? This was the second morning she'd been missing. And where was Mr. Elmer?

Margaret came trailing into the kitchen dragging a sheet. "Where's Mommy?"

"At the hospital having the baby, remember?"

"But that was way last night. This is morning. I want her."

"She won't be home for awhile; maybe this whole week. Mr. Elmer's coming."

"I want Mommy." Margaret began to whimper. Kate felt desperate. She put her arm about Margaret.

"She'll be home soon. Don't cry."

"I want her *now*," wailed Margaret. Kate felt tears coming. She wanted Dad . . . Mr. Elmer . . . Nathan . . . anyone to come and help. She wiped at her eyes.

"Race you upstairs to dress." Margaret was gone in an instant.

Kate talked nonsense and tickled her while they dressed. They made a game out of dismantling the tent and making the beds. When they went downstairs, Kate played one-handed jacks with Margaret and did it so clumsily that Margaret went off into gales of laughter.

"Is it lunch time?" Margaret asked.

Kate had forgotten that Margaret hadn't had breakfast. They went to the kitchen. Margaret pulled open the refrigerator. "Stinks," she said holding her nose. Kate looked in. She sniffed the milk. Sour. She ran to the front porch. No fresh bottles sat there in the box. Mr. Frizzell hadn't made his delivery. Slowly she returned to the kitchen. Margaret watched her solemnly. "Mommy," she said her face beginning to pucker.

Kate felt like crying too, but instead she began making a peanut butter and jelly sandwich. She mustn't let on to Margaret how she felt.

Margaret swung her legs, put her elbows on the table and took three big bites from the heart of each sandwich half. Kate watched her without seeing her. She wished violently that Mr. Elmer would come.

"Let's go outside," Margaret said.

"OK." Kate got up quickly. They put on their boots and raincoats. The slanty rain had almost stopped. Margaret dived for the puddles just as Josh had. Kate watched her, then walked to the edge of the road. The ditches were rushing streams. The new corn was flattened, and a triangular lake shimmered at the low corner of the field. Kate threaded her way across the debris-strewn yard toward the barn. Margaret ran up behind her. The cows stood at the door, heads down, dumb, waiting to be milked.

"I thought Mr. Elmer was coming to take care of us?"

"So did I," Kate answered.

"Hey, there's Blackie!" Margaret screamed. Blackie trotted across the lawn, jumping twigs and limbs, going toward the kitchen door.

"Blackie." Kate scooped her up and held her to her neck. She felt light and flabby. "You've had your babies." Blackie meowed, and Kate dropped her gently. They poured the sour milk into her bowl under the stove and crouched down to see if she would drink it. After one lick Blackie turned her head away. But she did eat all the spoiled stew. As soon as she finished, she went to the door.

"Let's follow her," Margaret whispered as they let her out. They stood on the porch watching. Blackie went into the garage and didn't come out. "Her babies must be in there," Margaret said.

"Must be," Kate answered. They began to look, but Margaret soon lost interest and ran back to her puddles. She made leaf boats, put a twig in each boat and crooned that they were kittens.

Kate stayed in the garage. Where could Blackie have gone? She looked everywhere; in the drawers of Dad's workbench, on the shelves above, even behind the hose he kept coiled against the wall. Finally she took a flashlight from its place in the tool box and crawled under the workbench. There was a jagged hole in the side wall. She lay flat and peered into the hole but couldn't see anything.

The storm had blown open the doors of the room where the Strawbridge carriage had once been kept. She went in and looked for the hole on the other side of the wall. But there was none. Puzzled, she returned to the garage and shined her light into the hole. She returned to the carriage room. No flashlight beam shone anywhere. Kate sat back on her heels and pulled her ear. Vague unconnected thoughts began to revolve in her head. Saturday . . . car . . . Sherlock . . . Dad . . . Norwood Builder . . . corridor . . . Norwood.

She got up, holding her head very still so that none of the confusing tangle would be disturbed. Car . . . Dad . . . Norwood Builder . . . too long . . . corridor . . .

As if in a trance she pressed herself against the end wall and stepped out, pacing the carriage room. 1—2—3—4—5—6—7—8—9—10—11—12—13—14—15—paces. She walked into the garage and paced it. 1—2—3—4—5—6—7—8—9—10—11—12—13—14—15—16—17—18—19—20—21—paces. She stood against the wall. Fifteen and twenty-one. Her head swam. She whirled, shook her head violently and then repaced the garage. It was still twenty-one. She flew to the carriage room next door and paced it. Fifteen again.

The garage was six paces longer than this old carriage room!

A strange feeling like yeast growing filled her stomach. She went to the end wall and knocked. Then she knocked on the side walls. She walked outside and round to the back. She knocked on the garage wall, then the carriage room wall. She retraced her steps and stared at the end wall of the carriage room. She went toward it and began feeling it all over. She had just crouched in the corner and was feeling along the floor when Margaret burst in. "Whatcha looking for?"

"Blackie," Kate said glibly.

"Come see my boats," Margaret said. Kate went, mind whirling. She stood on one foot, then the other, pretending interest in Margaret's fleet. "Now what'll I do?" Margaret asked.

"Build a bridge for them to sail under," Kate said quickly. She couldn't have Margaret tagging her *now*.

"How?"

Kate took a branch, stripped the leaves from it and arched it over the pond. "You can build a dock here and make a city there and . . ."

"I'll do it." Margaret pushed Kate away. Kate didn't give her a backward glance as she hurried back to the carriage room. She began running her hands over the wood of the back wall. It had wooden strips down it at regular intervals.

There must be some way to get to those six paces behind that wall!

Her hands flew hither and yon. Abruptly she stopped. Oscar would laugh at her helter-skelter approach. She moved deliberately to the left side of the wall and sank down in the very corner. She began to feel the wood, pressing, probing. She worked her way up the strip until she could reach no higher. She did this to every panel across the room. Then she got a small stepladder from the garage and set it in the right-hand corner. She climbed up, ready to continue.

The dark corner loomed above, cloudy with spiderwebs. She shuddered. She got a broom and brushed the ceiling as best she could. Then she climbed back onto the ladder and pressed her hand into the very corner.

Her heart stopped.

Something hard and cold met her fingers. She explored its shape. It was a bolt! She pulled at it with all her might, and finally it gave with a screech. The panel moved in. She leaped from the ladder and dropped to her knees, scrabbling frantically at the soft earth of the floor. With palsied fingers she uncovered a second bolt near the ground and shot it loose. The panel moved in again. She stared at it, her heart rocketing around in her chest. She stood up and pushed gently. The panel swung protestingly. She was about to step through the opening when a wail came from the yard. Frantically she slid the lower bolt into place and ran from the room.

"I got a splinter," Margaret cried sucking her finger. Kate tried to draw the splinter out, but her hands were shaking so that it broke off. Margaret jerked away. "You don't do it like Mommy," she cried. In the little bathroom off the den Kate daubed it with iodine, kissed it and wrapped it in a hanky.

"There. Mr. Elmer'll fix it better when he comes."

"When's he coming?"

"I don't know." Kate looked up at the clock on the kitchen wall. It still said 12:58.

"Bet he'll like my ships," Margaret said rushing back to her fleet. Kate stood poised. She flew to the phone. It was still dead. Then she raced up to her room and grabbed the yellow tablet. She had to tell *someone* about her discovery.

211261323 212615822 4261515 132237 712
20269262022 26 1526 81922915122416 19121514228.
1813 131294121223 256181523229. 20269262022
(21), 24269918262022 9121214 (15). 719181316
25152624161822 192623 16187722138 71922922.
2614 2231115129181320 91820197 13124. 8121422
719613232298712914, 19619?

14'1526232

She put a stamp on the envelope and flew to the big mailbox and raised the red flag. She stood by the box. Would Mr. Pumper come today? No cars passed, and she couldn't remember hearing any all day. No Mr. Frizzell, no Mr. Elmer, no Mr. Pumper. . . . She ran to the house, but she couldn't outrun her uneasiness.

She stopped at the sideboard and stuffed candles and matches into her raincoat and ran toward the garage-shed. Margaret was still occupied with her twig city and stick kittens and didn't look up as Kate went past.

Thoughts of Oscar sobered Kate. She returned the ladder to the garage, crawled under the workbench and pulled the flashlight from the hole. After putting it in its place, she went back to the carriage room where she shot the bolt and crouched before it. She lighted her candle with shaking fingers, pushed on the panel, hesitated an instant, then taking a gulp of air slipped sidewise through the opening. She thrust her candle out. Two ghostly yellow points of light swam in the mist before her.

# Chapter 15

She almost dropped the candle. A familiar grumble filled the darkness.

"Blackie," Kate breathed, relief pouring through her. Blackie's yellow eyes looked like saucers in the glare of the candle. Six wormlike kittens nursed at her belly. "So this is where you had your babies," Kate whispered. Blackie snarled. Kate drew back.

"I won't hurt them, I'm Kate, remember?" But Blackie's eyes remained wide and hostile. "If you're going to be like that," Kate tossed her head, "I won't even look at your silly old kittens."

Having Blackie there was reassuring. Kate began to look about the room. Across the two end walls were huge wooden cupboards. Kate opened one and a musty smell eddied into the little room. It was filled with long dresses. On the shelf above was a neat row of bonnets all with dark, concealing veils, and on the floor were two even rows of old-fashioned shoes and boots. The other cupboard had men's clothes. Several trunks were lined up against the wall. Blackie and her kittens lay on one that had somehow been left open.

Kate sat down abruptly, overwhelmed with her discovery. Just then Blackie shook free of her babies and disappeared behind the trunk. Kate leaned down with her candle. Blackie's entrance and exit was the jagged hole under the workbench.

Kate stopped short. If Margaret saw Blackie, she'd come nosing around here—she had to head her off. She left the secret room quickly, pulled the panel shut and slipped out of the carriage room. But Margaret wasn't in the yard. Kate called and called, then she went into the house. Margaret lay asleep on the couch in her wet raincoat.

What unexpected luck. She could explore undetected for at least an hour.

She tiptoed to the back door and was just about to go out when she stopped. Three hobos were rounding the lilac bushes and coming straight for the back door. Kate stood paralyzed for an instant; then she pushed the heavy door closed and locked it. She crept into the den and stood concealed behind the curtain, staring out at the three shabby men. The hobos pounded on the door. Kate shuddered. They pounded again. Then they looked in the kitchen window. Kate ducked below the windowsill and crouched there, trembling. They were talking among themselves, but Kate couldn't make out their words. Then silence. Fearfully she peeked over the windowsill. They were gone.

She was still shaking as she went to the sideboard and stuffed more candles and matches into her pockets. It was several minutes before she got up enough courage to unlock the door and run back to the carriage room. But the minute she entered, excitement took hold of her again. She pushed the panel in and shut it firmly. She lit a candle, then leaned over the trunk and lifted a tiny kitten to her cheek. It was so soft and small . . . the trunk wobbled as she leaned against it. She put the kitten down and looked at the unsteady trunk. She rocked it gently back and forth. Then she pushed it with all her might to see what was under it.

It was a rusty ring!

She closed her eyes, counted to ten, opened them. The rusty ring was still there. Her hand went out of its own accord and touched it. The kittens squeaked and nosed about blindly. Dreams didn't have squeaking kittens in them.

She reached out and pulled. Dirt slid from the small trap door as she pulled up. Slowly it opened. With a gasp she let it fall back. She leaned forward and looked down into a dark hole. Rolling onto her stomach she lowered the candle as far as she could.

The hole went straight down, lined with smooth stones. On one side were semicircular iron rods fastened into the stones like steps. It looked like a well . . . with steps. Kate lay panting, her candle shaking.

LIBERTY WELL . . . ROUND STEPS . . .

A wildness took hold of her. She dropped one of her candle stubs into the hole. It landed with a faint thud. A well, but no water. Blackie leaped back to her kittens. With Blackie here, nothing could happen to her. All caution left Kate. She put her foot on the top iron step and went down.

The bottom came sooner than she expected. Quickly she lighted a candle. The flame was steady and even. Eagerly she turned around.

There was a door!

. . . ROUND STEPS, THEN THE LABYRINTH . . .

What was behind that door? She lighted two more candles and stuck them into the soft earth so she could see, then seized the latch and pushed the door open. Air moved against her face and a peculiar undefinable odor came rushing past her. The candle flame wavered. A narrow passageway led off into the gloom. Kate never hesitated. Heedlessly she let go of the door and rushed down the passageway toward the smell. She lifted her candle high.

Before her yawned a huge emptiness. She moved forward . . . THEN THE LABYRINTH . . . It was an-

160

other natural HALL, all right, but this HALL had more than empty boxes in it. Tables, benches, beds, dishes, rugs, and even a rocking chair. Kate leaped about the room looking, poking. Her finger went through the rotting fabric of a pillow, and bits of feather drifted weirdly in the cold, smelly air. She fingered the blankets, and they became dust in her hands. The mattresses rustled as she touched them. Candle holders were everywhere, tallow drips thick on the table. Was it the wax that smelled so? She peered into the crocks and took one of the metal mugs in her hand. She sat on the benches, in the rocking chair. As she sat rocking, she looked about. In the corner was a huge pile of barrels.

. . . TRUTH AND FREEDOM . . . HIDDEN FROM FALSE MEN . . .

The slaves had been hidden here in this part of the LABYRINTH, then the Strawbridges had taken them up the LIBERTY WELL, dressed them in disguises and had driven them to the docks in the carriage.

Suddenly she *had* to tell Oscar.

Seizing the candle she dived up the passage. The door was closed. She pushed it. It didn't open. She threw herself against it. Still it didn't open. With unsteady fingers she felt for an inside latch. There was none, just smooth, solid wood. She put her candle on the floor and looked apprehensively at the door. There had to be an inside latch. Distraught, she

*161*

examined the door again.

Her bravado vanished. She began pounding with her cast, screaming for Dad . . . Mr. Elmer . . . Margaret . . . Blackie. . . . Hysterically she threw herself against the door again and again, shouting, crying, blubbering, until her knees buckled and she slumped over in a heap. An uncontrollable shaking took hold of her.

How long she lay there she never knew, but gradually she stopped shaking. The fog of fear began to lift from her brain. What would Oscar do? . . .

She sat staring at the flame of the candle. Finally she pulled herself to her feet and returned to the slave room. She took one of the three kitchen chairs and propped it against the door, then mounted it and began to examine the door a third time.

A needle of hope pricked her. There was a narrow open slot across the top of the door, and through it she could see the light of the two candles she had left on the floor of the well. She turned her head sidewise and tried to push it through the slot. It wouldn't go. She began to shout again. Someone had to hear her. She shouted until she was hoarse.

Silence.

She gave the entire door an Oscar-like examination . . . careful, meticulous, slow. At intervals she shouted through the slot. But at last she finished her search and went into the slave room and slumped

down in the rocking chair. She rocked a little, afraid to recognize the certainty that was growing in her.

She was trapped!

She spilled her candles and matches onto the rug before her. Nine candle stubs and twenty-eight matches. Could she burn the door down? No, too much smoke . . . she'd suffocate. Oscar . . . sensible Oscar. . . . He wouldn't have gotten himself into a fix like this. If only she'd been more sensible. . . .

She flew out of the rocker, up the short corridor toward the door, and stopped before it. Then she took a deep breath. Hadn't she pushed the door *in* when she had first entered the passageway?

She climbed onto the chair, stuck her good arm through the slot, and pushed with all her might. The door didn't budge. She blew out her candle, dropped the smoking stub to the floor, and gingerly eased her cast through the slot. Now she could push with both arms. But the door remained firmly closed as before.

Then she knew. The latch had closed, and no amount of pushing would free her.

Yet she couldn't accept the fact. It just couldn't be . . . no inside latch. All doors had *two* latches. . . . She stopped and let her breath out in a long sigh. Of course . . . to keep the slaves safe. If a slave had gotten out and been seen, then the Strawbridge station would have been worthless. She looked at the top again. If only that slot were bigger . . . if only she had an ax . . . if only. . . .

She stepped from the chair and picked up her candle stub and lighted it. She then went into the slave HALL searching for something sharp . . . anything. Knives. She seized two and ran back to the door. She began to saw away at the top of the door. But the door was an inch thick, and the knife only tickled the wood. Doggedly she sawed away.

The flickering light beyond the slot went out. Her one candle now was all she had against the immense blackness that pressed around her. Shaking, she held the candle to the indentation she had made in the door. It was tiny. Despondent, she dropped the knives. It would take a year to get out that way.

A year? Her stomach rumbled. All the times she'd chided Oscar for his caution and good sense returned to haunt her. She swayed back and forth, her mind a cauldron of half-thoughts, promises, recriminations, reforms . . . prayers. Dear God, get me out of here.

She began shouting again. But when she stopped to listen, there was nothing but that terrible silence again. If only Blackie would come down the well so she could tie a message to her neck . . . if Margaret would look under Dad's workbench and find the hole. . . .

The candle sputtered and went out. Utter darkness swallowed her up. She fumbled in her pocket for her candles. . . . It was empty. Where? . . . Then she remembered. She had put the candles and matches on the rug before the rocker while she counted them.

How could she go in there . . . into that black void that smelled like a tomb. . . . She quivered on the chair, arguing with herself. Then the chair wobbled and she jumped off. Before she could think, she edged along the wall to the end of the passage and felt her way to the rocker. With blind hands she patted the rug. At last her fingers encountered the little pile of stubs and matches. She scratched a match. The flame flared, she held it to the black wick. The candle glow pushed the darkness back and her agitated breathing began to subside.

How many candles? Eight left. She measured each. All the stubs were about three inches long. How long did it take a candle to burn an inch? How long did she have before the inevitable blackness of the slave HALL would engulf her for good? The thought was too much, and her mind began to revolve like a berserk merry-go-round. Motto . . . Oscar . . . Dad . . . motto . . . dead. . . .

She shrieked, leaped up and stamped her foot. "Kate, you aren't going to die. Think . . . think, Kate. . . ." The berserk merry-go-round swung with her words. She stamped her foot again, then raced to the blank door. The knives lay where she had dropped them, but they were too puny, and she rushed back to the room searching for something bigger, something to get her out of here. But she found nothing.

The merry-go-round whirled wickedly. She jumped onto the wobbly chair and it collapsed under her. She crashed to the floor, but she was too upset to stop and rub her bruises. She raced back and got another chair. She sprang up on it with her knife and attacked the door wildly. She sawed and shouted, shouted and sawed. At last she became too weary to lift her arm. She took her almost-gutted candle and returned to the slave HALL, where she eased the light into a holder. Then recklessly she lit two more candles and jammed them into other holders. She put them on the table, then pulled two mattresses together, found a quilt that hadn't gone to dust, and lay down. The light was so pleasant . . . warm . . . steady . . . living. . . .

An exhausted sleep overwhelmed her, and all three priceless candles burned on and on and on until their wicks were drowned in hot wax and they sputtered out forever.

# Chapter 16

Kate opened her eyes. Blackness . . . catastrophic blackness. . . . Her damp clothes clammed against her skin, and her hands and feet were icy. A quivering started deep inside her. She closed her eyes and prayed rapidly, but her mind blurred, and she lost the thread of her prayer.

Her eyes rolled open again. Open . . . closed . . . the dark was the same. In slow motion she sat up, crawled across the rug and found a match. It didn't want to light because it was damp. At last . . . the tiny flame thrilled Kate as nothing ever had before. She sank back, lighted a candle and cupped her hands around the living flame.

She sneezed. The flame vanished. She sneezed so many times she lost count, then the hiccoughs started. She struck another precious match and lighted her candle again. Stiffly she got up. Then she saw what she had done . . . the three holders festooned with cold wax. The hiccoughs didn't prevent the tears. Hopelessness crowded her heart and brain, and her sobs filled the huge dark HALL.

Finally her self-pity spent itself and with a fierce movement she smeared away the tears with her sleeve, put her candle into a holder and knelt on the rug. Five stubs. What would Oscar do? . . . Dashing to the door, she flung herself onto the chair and began screaming through the slot. "Oscar . . . hic . . . I'm here . . . down . . . hic . . . here . . . come get me . . . God . . . make . . . Oscar . . . hic . . . find . . . me. . . ." She swooped down on the abandoned knives, took one and sawed senselessly at the tiny notch. The knife snapped in two. Without hesitating she gouged the broken half into the little hole, twisting, grinding. A trickle of sawdust dribbled to the floor. The knife shattered in her hand. She raced back to the slave HALL and got every utensil she could find and dumped them in the passageway, then assaulted the notch again. Just a small hole, not much, God, just a very small hole. . . .

The candle burned lower. How long . . . burn an inch? She jumped down and returned to the rug where her five remaining treasures lay. She sat down cross-legged before them. She'd already used half her supply. Before she could argue with herself she blew the candle out. The darkness fell in on her, and she felt as if she were being smothered. But rallying her

*169*

courage, she got up and felt her way to the door. Her fingers found the knife, she mounted the chair and felt for the notch, began to gouge again. Twist . . . turn . . . shout . . . listen . . . twist . . . turn. . . .

She felt her way off the chair, lighted the candle, and held it to the hole. Her confidence washed away in more tears, and she crawled back to her mattress and buried her face in the curve of her elbow. Her body shook. The candle burned . . . like life slipping away. Gradually the tears faded, and she began to repeat the motto over and over slowly, filling her mind with words to keep from thinking of. . . . Then abruptly she sat up.

"I won't . . . I won't! . . ." she yelled, shaking her fist in the air. "I won't die. I'll get out, you'll see . . . all of you . . . God . . . Dad . . . Oscar . . . the whole lot of you. You just wait, I'll get out. . . ." She dived at the door and began her gouging again. She twisted the knife so violently that it shattered. Two more disintegrated in her hand before she drew back to measure the hole. The jagged groove she had made across the top of the door was about an inch wide and half an inch deep.

She shouted . . . listened . . . then returned to her task. She blew out the candle and worked in the appalling darkness for what she thought was forever. At last she relighted the candle, looked at the hole. She told herself it was bigger, but she felt so discouraged that she could barely shout through the slot. "Oscar . . . Dad . . . find me . . . I'm down here . . . here . . . find me . . . Oscar . . . Oscar. . . ."

They must be looking for her. She'd been down here forever it seemed. She climbed off the chair and returned to the slave HALL. Shadows flickered weirdly on the rock walls. She sat for a long dull time, unmoving.

The shadows on the walls . . . odd shapes . . . dark and light. She lay back, put her arm under her head and began to make shapes out of the shadows. One looked like the spot of white on Blackie's forehead, another looked like a capital *T*, and yet another looked a bit like a bear. She played her idiotic game, wasting her candle, unable to stop.

She sneezed. "Dad . . . find me . . . please, Dad . . . ask Oscar. . . ." She bolted upright. The letter! Once Oscar got her letter he'd tell Dad and . . . and . . . once Dad knew about the false wall he'd come to find her. . . . She shouted the old hymn "Brighten the Corner Where You Are" at the top of her lungs. Mr. Pumper would deliver her letter and . . . and. . . . But the storm . . . no cars on the road . . . no milk. . . . She laughed at her fears, but the echoes mocked her. She stuck out her tongue at her prison. "I'll get out . . . just you wait and see. I *won't* die. I won't, I won't! Oscar and

God and Dad . . . they'll find me."

Her renewed faith sent her flying to her groove again. She shouted and gouged. Any minute now Dad and Oscar would be coming. She whooped louder. "Dad . . . Oscar . . . here . . . right here . . . it's so easy . . . I'm right down here in the LIBERTY WELL."

She worked and probed, yelling, singing, stopping to listen, screaming, pounding with her cast. "Dad . . . Oscar . . . Dad . . . Oscar. . . ." It became a litany.

Her confidence slid away as abruptly as it had come. She slouched to her mattress, lit another candle, stared lethargically at the shadows on the walls. She began repeating the motto over and over . . . over . . . and . . . over. . . .

She must have slept, for when she moved, her damp clothes were like a shroud. Her stuffed-up head throbbed, and she sneezed several times. Hunger was real and huge inside her. She swallowed, and her dry throat felt raspy. Automatically she began repeating the motto, but it had lost its magic. Her spirit was gone. Fumbling for a match she lighted a candle. Why save them? No use. She lay listlessly, her mind flitting from half-thought to half-thought. Dad . . . food . . . trapped . . . water . . . Oscar . . . death. . . .

"Why me? What did I do, God?" She cried until she couldn't cry any longer. Her fourth-to-last candle was almost gone. Surely by now Oscar had gotten her letter.

No Mr. Elmer . . . no milk . . . 12:58. . . .

Soberly she looked about, selected a rusty plate and scratched "Kate" on it with a stone. She threw it through the slot. To make sure she scratched three more plates and dropped them also. She shouted as best she could with her dry throat, listened, shouted again, then dug at the groove. Her head felt light as cotton, her stomach like an empty hole, her throat like a rusty pipe. She dug mindlessly at the hole. She had to get out of here . . . had to get out . . . get out. . . .

She blew out the candle and gouged at the little V in the door with every utensil until they all splintered and became useless. Finally she relit the candle and measured the groove. A despair so complete and ugly that she could taste it overpowered her. She shuffled back into the slave HALL, fell into the rocker and moaned. Rocking and moaning, rocking and moaning. The candle burned down. The shadows flickered on the uneven walls. Flickered . . . like the shadows on the walls of the other HALL that she had found. . . . This HALL was bigger than the HALL that she and Oscar had found . . . much bigger. And no HALL-in blocking the way. She moaned. If only there

173

*had* been a HALL-in . . . or something to have made her stop and consider. . . . Her head seemed to lift off her shoulders and move about the room. It was nodding and smiling and talking. It was repeating the motto, over and over:

THEN THE LABYRINTH
TRUTH AND FREEDOM
HIDDEN FROM FALSE MEN
EMPTY IT SEEMS
BUT THEREIN LIES THE TALE

. . . THEN THE LABYRINTH . . . THEN THE LABYRINTH . . . was one HALL a labyrinth?

She got up, reached for her detached head and put it back on her shoulders. She staggered to the wall and began to feel the stones. Then, feebly, she remembered Oscar, and she moved to the door and began on the right. Her hand grew numb from the icy rocks. So cold. The candle in her cast hand was an unsteady light. Poke, thrust . . . every shadow could lead to the LABYRINTH.

Occasionally she crawled to the door to shout and listen, but now she knew that was just a ritual.

She inched around the huge HALL. So tired. . . . She looked around the room. Half-done. Doggedly she forced her cold tired arm up. The flame wavered, but she couldn't tell if it was the air or her arm trembling. She slid over a pile of rocks and peered behind a huge boulder. It was very dark behind there . . . very . . . empty? She squeezed past the boulder and pushed her candle before her.

Irrepressible hope rose in her again. She moved too quickly, fell. Her candle disappeared between two rocks and went out, but she didn't care.

The LABYRINTH was out there!

She rubbed her bruised knees, got up and felt her way back to the rug. She lighted her third-to-last candle, stuffed the remaining two and the matches into her pocket, and was just about to start for the exit when she stopped in her tracks.

What if her letter to Oscar had been delivered, Dad and Oscar were coming, and when they got here, she was gone? . . .

What should she do . . . go or stay? An amorphous feeling said go, but could she trust her judgment? What would Oscar do? With a quick puff she blew out the candle and sat down on the rug. Oscar wouldn't waste candle power, of that she was certain.

Now, to be sensible, like Oscar. First she'd think out all the reasons for going . . . then the reasons for staying. . . . A feeling of weakness enveloped her. Water . . . if only she had a sip of water . . . she could think . . . think like Oscar. . . . Languidly she extended her forefinger.

Point one: If she plunged into the LABYRINTH as

heedlessly as she'd plunged through the well door
. . . well . . . water . . . in a worse fix than now.
Stay here. . . . She sighed heavily. First she had to
list all the reasons for *going*. Maybe if she said them
out loud. "If I say herer, tey coul comm ust atter I
lef. . . ." Her sandpaper tongue clacked about in her
parched mouth. Her rusty throat contracted. Water
. . . just a sip. Dad, Oscar . . . come . . . soon
. . . so thirsty. . . .

Back to Point one. If she plunged into the
LABYRINTH . . . Lake Erie, water everywhere . . .
mustn't think about that . . . LABYRINTH . . . go
or stay . . . long down here . . . day . . . three
days . . . week. . . .

Go to sleep . . . Dad . . . find her . . . take
care of her . . . sleep . . . no . . . mustn't . . .
make trail . . . go . . . thirsty . . . must move
. . . go. . . .

Like a sleepwalker she lighted her candle, felt to be
sure all her matches and candles were in her pocket,
then she forced herself to her feet. She grabbed the
table for support. With a stone she scratched "Kate"
on four plates and stuffed them under her arm. Then
she stumbled toward the opening behind the boulder.
At the exit she left a plate where it would be visible
to anyone entering the HALL, then went slowly
behind the boulder and down the passageway.

It was fairly straight and dry. Kate limped along

as best she could. At least she was doing something. The tunnel sloped down. She tried to hurry, but she fell. Her candle went out. With a great effort she found it and lighted it again. How long she sat staring at the flame she didn't know, but after a long time she forced herself to her knees. A dizziness gripped her, and the tunnel tilted as she fell again. She lay on her side, unable to move, but she still clutched her lighted candle. Finally she forced herself to her knees . . . then her feet. Steadying herself against the rocky wall of the tunnel, she concentrated grimly. This tunnel . . . was just like the tunnels in the caves she'd explored with Dad out on the lake bluffs. Maybe she'd come out there . . . on the lake edge . . . water . . . all of the lake to drink . . . no . . . mustn't think . . . this HALL . . . connected to lake HALLS. . . . She thrust out her candle and moved down the wall. Just ahead the tunnel widened, then divided into three separate tunnels. She moved forward, every step a painful effort. She flashed the candle into the entrance of the first corridor, the second, the last.

A scream rose in her throat, but no sound issued from her dehydrated lips. Was it real . . . a real . . . like the others . . . box. . . . As if in a dream she moved toward it. It was exactly like the others she and Oscar had found in their LABYRINTH. She stared down at the box. It was wedged between some stones in such a way that it seemed to point down the left corridor. Was it happenstance that it lay at that peculiar angle or? . . . She looked and looked at the box, then down the left corridor. She tried to think about the boxes that she and Oscar had found. So long ago . . . had they been in special places where tunnels divided? Not the first one, of course, for it had been in HALL, but the others? . . . How many . . . where? . . . She sank down on the frigid stones. Her brain didn't want to work. Boxes . . . tunnels dividing . . . there . . . where? . . . Her brain remained frozen, but a prickle of hopefulness penetrated her lethargy. She lifted the box and shook it feebly. Something shifted inside. The prickle spread through her arms and legs and she clamped the box under her cast, left a plate at the entrance to the left corridor, and started down the new tunnel. It wound down, then up, finally straightened out. She went so slowly . . . the tunnel stretched on and on . . . and on . . . then it began to wind. . . .

The hope and energy generated by the box dwindled away. She prayed without faith. The length of her candle and one more stub was the margin of her life. When they went out. . . . She crumpled to the floor. Rest . . . just for a minute . . . the candle slipped from her hand and the flame died.

When she woke she still clutched the box. Her stomach had disappeared and only a terrible aching remained. Her tongue was like a gag. She tried to stand up, but the dizziness overwhelmed her and she fell back. She lay for a long, long time. Somewhere in her being she knew she had to get up or die. Forgetting about the candle stub among the stones, she lighted her last candle. It took all her strength and willpower. She cupped her frozen hands about the small warmth and shivered. The flame became the center of her universe. When it went out . . . so would she. . . .

At last she pushed herself up, holding onto the wall for support, shaking away the faintness that threatened to beat her to the floor again. Hardly knowing what she was doing, she staggered down the corridor, the box clamped to her side.

. . . LABYRINTH . . . under whole crazy town . . . no way out . . . Injun Joe. . . motto . . . lured her into these trackless . . . LABYRINTH . . . one foot . . . other . . . foot . . . left . . . right . . . cold . . . water . . . so cold . . . was Heaven warm?

One foot . . . then the other. It was all she could do to just keep moving one foot after the other. The candle flame grew taller and taller, wavering dramatically. Candle was dying. Mom said once that

dying was like going to sleep. One foot . . . the
other . . . warm . . . water. . . .

The corridor divided. She looked stupidly from one
tunnel to the other. Listlessly she looked at the floor
for the box to tell her which way to go. Her eyes
blurred . . . blinked . . . blurred. . . .

Something white snaked through the stones and
pebbles of the floor.

Then from somewhere came the echo of Oscar's
voice.

"It's *my* string, and I said *leave* it. That way we'll
know which passages we've explored."

Her numb brain couldn't think, but she fixed her
eyes on the string and set one foot . . . then the
other . . . left . . . right. . . . The candle sputtered.
She plodded on, never lifting her eyes from that
white line. It wound on and on and mesmerized, she
followed. Oscar's string . . . lead . . . HALL . . .
WATER BUG . . . home . . . water. . . . Her being
stirred and she dared begin to hope. Coming . . .
coming . . . Oscar . . . Dad . . . coming . . .
wait . . . water . . . water . . . left . . . right
. . . faster . . . faster . . . faster. . . . Stumbling
and wheezing she pressed on. The candle flame
smoked and flickered. A current of air moved against
her face. HALL . . . HALL . . . HALL . . . coming
. . . HALL. . . .

At last . . . at last. . . . She burst into the big

room. There was the end of Oscar's string tied about the rock. Wonderful Oscar. . . . She rushed, fell, pushed herself to her knees and crawled to the water jar. It was empty.

Hurry . . . river . . . water. . . . She picked up a flashlight, and the incredibly bright beam made her blink. She dropped her candle and crawled to the passageway around the HALL-in. Her heart thundered in her chest. Coming . . . river . . . water . . . The panel was open, for they'd rushed out the last time they'd been here, and then Mom had forbidden. . . . Water. . . . Kate wavered to her feet . . . hurry . . . water . . . coming. . . . In blind haste she floundered through the shaft. Water . . . water. . . . The shaft became lower, but she didn't remember . . . she crashed into a supporting beam. . . . No sound came as she crumpled into unconsciousness, but the beam of her flashlight shined brightly out the entrance that led to freedom . . . and water.

# Chapter 17

Heaven *was* warm . . . one side of her was burning up. She shifted uneasily.

"Hey, she moved."

"Maybe she's comin' round." Two shadows appeared through her eyelids. Kate raised a hand that weighed a ton to her eyes. Her swollen tongue lay in her mouth like a great furry egg.

"Poor little tyke. Wonder how she got in there in the first place, and wonder what's in that box she won't let go of?"

"Cxu . . . pxzt . . ."

"She's trying to say somethin'. Get that rag out of that can of water, Pete." Something marvelously wet entered her mouth. She sucked frantically. Her eyelids slowly opened and she focused on the two shadows.

Then an unreasoning fear exploded through her. She tried to roll away, but a fierce pain shot through her forehead. Sinister hands held her down. She moaned piteously and rolled her head away from the two hobos who leaned threateningly over her.

Water splashed into her mouth, ran down her cheeks and neck. Her swollen tongue swam in it. She gagged . . . coughed . . . choked. . . .

"Not that much, Pete . . . she'll drown. Must have been in that cave a long time to get that dried out. Keep that rag wet . . . that's about all she can manage just now." Kate chewed on the wet rag and sucked and sucked. "Easy does it, kid," one of the hobos said kindly. Such an awful headache . . . box under her cast . . . hadn't stolen it from her. . . . Her panic eased, but her head throbbed as her arm had when she'd first broken it.

"Bet she's starving too. You got anything on you, Pete?"

"Not a crust."

"Me neither. Haven't eaten since Cleveland. . . ." At least they didn't want her for dessert.

"Wonder who she is . . . and what's in that box?"

"Give her a while on that rag and she'll tell us." Kate watched them from under her weighted eyelids. If they were like Mr. Lord? . . .

"Pooxz . . . bppwc . . . rzqtyp . . . wszz. . . ." Her tongue was still stiff and fat as Blackie's "mad" tail.

"Just give yourself time, kid," Pete said gently.

"Me and my friend here, we'll take care of you and your old box and get you home safe and sound. Don't know how you got yourself into that cave, but we got you out, didn't we, Oscar?"

Kate's eyes flickered at the mention of Oscar's name. They saw it. "Oscar . . . that name means somethin' to you . . . don't it? He your dad?" Kate could barely move her aching head to nod no. "Your brother . . . uncle . . . friend. . . ." At the last word Kate nodded yes weakly.

"Now you got two friends named Oscar," Pete said very gently. "Oscar here, he found the cave. We saw that beam of light . . . spookiest thing I ever saw; but Oscar here, he got right up and went a-runnin' toward that light and up to it like he was a moth. And there was this big hole and the light a-shinin' out of it. And there you was, lyin' on the floor in there. Oscar dragged you out, and we brung you down here and has been warmin' you up by the fire for an hour now. . . . Don't you worry about a thing, me and Oscar here, we'll take care of you." Then forgetting himself he asked, "How'd you get yourself lost in there in the first place?"

"She can't talk yet," Oscar said. "We have to ask questions she can nod to . . . like . . . you live around here?"

Kate barely inclined her head.

"You want us to take you home?" Kate inclined

her head again. She tried to get up, but she fell back gasping. "We'll have to carry her," Oscar said to Pete. "She's some sick kid."

They made a chair for her by clasping their wrists with their hands. They had to lift her into the chair and Pete put her free arm about his neck. In the other she still clasped the box. The two hobos pushed their way through the underbrush until they came to the path.

"Hey, lookit this." Kate indicated the way with an outstretched foot. It took a long time to get to the steps. When they came to the place where the steps started up, Kate stuck her foot out again. They couldn't carry her up the steep bank between them, so Oscar knelt down and Pete laid Kate on his back. She hung on with one arm, for she wouldn't let go of the box. It was a tortuous climb, but somehow they reached the top and all three fell full length in the pasture grass, panting and exhausted.

Kate's eyes turned toward the house. Was it still there? The barn loomed darkly across the pasture, and the house sparkled behind, lights radiating from every window. Kate stared, too weak and bewildered to believe. She pointed to the house.

"Must be where she lives," Pete said sitting up.

"Glad it ain't no farther," Oscar said. He and Pete made the chair again and got Kate into it. They struggled across the pasture. Kate watched the golden house advance. Please, God . . . not a dream. . . .

Two cars stood in the driveway; the limousine and a new Ford sedan with SHERIFF in gold letters on each front door.

"Hey, Oscar, I ain't hankerin' to meet no sheriff. . . ." Pete gasped almost collapsing under Kate's slight weight.

"Pipe down. He won't throw us in the clink once he hears we've found this kid. . . ." They banged on the door, but no one came. Kate's heart contracted. It was a dream after all . . . the house was a silent shell.

"What in the h—?" Oscar began. Just then there was a great burst of noise from around the house. Pete and Oscar turned toward it. With their last strength they carried Kate toward the garage-shed where light angled out over the lawn from the carriage room.

"That's the wall, Mr. Cummings." Oscar's voice came high and clear from the carriage room. A splintering smash followed.

"Almost!" Nathan yelled.

"Again, Edgar, again!" Mrs. Witherspoon urged.

"Come on, Dad, once more's got it!" Josh shouted.

The hobos staggered into the light with Kate. They stopped perplexed by the confusion before them. Two powerful flashlights, held by Sheriff Popcorne and his ancient deputy, Sergeant Stonegrave, illuminated Dad who stood poised at the gashed false wall, an ax

swung far back over his head. Grouped about either side were Mrs. Witherspoon, Oscar, Simone, Nathan, Margaret, Josh, Mr. Elmer and Flint, all yelling, gesticulating, giving advice. Dad swung the ax from his heels and hit the false wall with a second rending crash.

Oscar and Pete looked on dumbly. Kate tried to call out, but nothing came out. Dad sent a third great ax blow to the wall and two panels collapsed. A mad ball of black fury sprang to his shoulder, spitting and snarling.

"Blackie!" Josh yelled. Blackie leaped toward the door, claws out. Everyone whirled.

"Kate!" Simone shrieked. Dad spun around, took four giant strides and seized Kate from the hobos' arms. For the third time in her life, Kate lost consciousness.

# *Chapter 18*

When she came to, she was lying in Dad's lap. A circle of faces wavered around her, and Sheriff Popcorne was shining his flashlight in her face. The rag still drooped from her mouth, and she clutched the box.

"That's her, all right," the sheriff boomed.

"Where'd you find her?" Dad looked at the two hobos suspiciously.

"In a cave. . . ." Pete began.

"When?"

"Couple of hours ago."

"God be praised!" Dad hugged her convulsively and rushed off across the lawn toward the house. Everyone ran after him. Sheriff Popcorne and Sergeant Stonegrave herded Pete and Oscar before them. Kate felt herself being laid on the couch. "Watch her, Elizabeth. I'm calling Doc Marsh this minute."

Mrs. Witherspoon knelt down in a flutter of skirts and the smell of lilacs and began chafing Kate's cold thin hand. "There, there, it's all right now. Those hobos can't hurt you any more."

"You bums say you found her in a *cave?*" Sheriff Popcorne accused. "No caves in these parts . . . only out along the lake. You find her way out there?" Pete and Oscar edged away from him.

"Naw, down by the river."

"River?" the sheriff exploded. "Talk fast, fellows, 'cause you're going to be in big trouble, and I mean *big* trouble iffen you don't tell the truth. There ain't no caves down the river way, least not that I ever heard tell of."

Pete began to talk fast. "Osc and me here, we was mindin' our own business there under the trestle when this here light pops on just up the riverbank. We sat there lookin' at it and a-wonderin' what it was. Then Osc here, he jumps up like goblins was after him and rushes off toward that light. And we find this here cave and this kid unconscious on the ground just inside. . . ."

"You know she's been missing for three whole days?" Popcorne stuck his chin into their faces. "You know that . . . three whole days? We was all set to drag the river tomorrow. . . ."

"We just found her, mister, honest. We just found her a little while ago. We ain't done nothin' to her."

Dad came bursting back into the living room.

"Doc says bring her straight down to the hospital. He'll meet us there."

"Flint," Mrs. Witherspoon commanded. Dad eased the box from Kate's grip, and Oscar hobbled forward and took it. Kate smiled at him with her eyes. Simone and Josh glared at him jealously. Then Dad lifted her very gently in his arms and went out to the limousine. Mrs. Witherspoon accompanied him, but all the others remained behind.

At the hospital Kate was whisked away to a bed, undressed and poked with a long hypodermic needle. Dad and Mrs. Witherspoon stood at the bottom of her bed smiling and saying soothing things, but soon they became fuzzy and faded away.

When she woke, her tongue was unstuck. Tentatively she moved it about in her mouth. She said, "Secret . . . Strawbridge Place. . . ." and it came out right. Even her stomach felt almost right. But she was awfully thirsty. She lay in the white hospital ward watching the nurses move about, feeling numb. There were tubes sticking in her arms.

People kept drifting by her bed and peering at her. They whispered and pointed at her, and then moved on. At last Dad came and smoothed the hair from her cheek. "Why's everyone staring at me?" she asked. Dad sat down on the edge of the bed.

"I'm afraid you've become a celebrity. The *Cleveland News* even had a story on your disappearance this morning. Everyone's mighty glad you aren't de . . . that is . . . not kidnapped or anything like that, so people are bound to stare. You set Ashtabula on its ear, my girl, and. . . ." But Kate broke in weakly.

"Mom?"

"She's fine, honey . . . now. We had a devil of a time that night getting to the hospital. You remember that storm, don't you? Well, a big tree blew down just in front of the car, scared your mom half to death. I had to carry her the rest of the way to the hospital through that downpour, and she got chilled. She hemorrhaged, and I had to stay close by. Phones were out, so never did call Mr. Elmer. It was the next day before your mom was out of danger, and I staggered home. There was Margaret crying to beat the band saying that you'd hidden from her and wouldn't come. Then Nathan and Josh came from the shop, and we all called and looked for you, but you'd vanished into thin air. I almost went crazy thinking about you and Margaret out home alone, and those hobos coming to the door asking for handouts . . . I thought you'd been kidnapped or . . . something worse. So I called Sheriff Popcorne, and he came soon as he could. He was frantic with all the roads being blocked by trees down and floods and wires down everywhere. That was some storm. He searched with us for awhile, then rounded up the hobos that were in the camp under the trestle and grilled them, but they didn't know anything so he had to let them go. Mr. Elmer finally got through the high water and came, and we searched again. Popcorne got the story into the *Ashtabula Sentinal*, and they ran a big picture on the front page; and so the next day the whole town was looking for you. I was going cuckoo, your mom so sick and you gone. The hospital and I, we managed to keep it from her . . . she doesn't know yet that you were missing and have been found. . . ."

"But she's OK for sure?"

"Right as rain." Dad hugged her. "But she'll be in the hospital for awhile."

"The baby?" Kate hardly dared ask.

"Twins," Dad smiled. "A boy and a girl. They're fine. It's just your mom who's having problems." Kate almost burst with relief.

"And Oscar and Pete?"

"Sheriff Popcorne was pretty suspicious of them at first, then they showed us the cave where they found you. And we explored it and eventually came up and explored the false room and the LIBERTY WELL and the slave room and saw where you'd been and all that. We found the plates that you'd scratched. So

Pete and Oscar are at the mansion. Old Man Porch said they were both heroes and gave them each a job."

Kate said nothing. She couldn't, she was too happy. If only she could drink up Lake Erie, she'd be right as rain herself.

She was in the hospital four days, then Dad came and took her home. Mrs. Witherspoon and Flint appeared as Dad carried her through the crowd of nurses and orderlies who clustered along the halls. The name "Witherspoon" and "Cummings kid" rippled among them as they watched. But Kate was used to all the attention by now. She'd heard herself described as "that little Cummings kid who'd been found in a cave by two bums and who'd had her picture in the *Sentinal* twice and the *Cleveland News* once, and on the front page all three times." Kate waved and smiled shyly at the nurses, and they waved back. Then Flint settled them in the car and closed the door, and the limousine rolled away.

As they turned in the drive, Josh and Simone swooped onto the running boards shouting. Oscar stood in the middle of the drive, his arms out like a stop sign. Nathan held Margaret by the hand to keep her from rushing to the car. Mr. Elmer stood on the porch and spit. Dad lifted Kate out and carried her onto the couch and spread an afghan over her. "Welcome home, Kate." He couldn't stop smiling. Mr. Elmer brought in a tray of lemonade and handed the glasses around.

Kate looked around her eagerly. There were so many things she didn't know. Oscar downed his lemonade in two gulps and stood poised, bursting with questions. But before he could open his mouth, Margaret rushed to the couch. "Kate, you're bad. You ran away and hid and made me cry."

Kate closed her eyes and remembered back over the eternity of time since the storm.

"Oh, Margaret." She held out her arms. "I didn't mean to hide. It just happened. . . ." She stopped. Everyone waited. "You see, while you were playing in the puddles, I found this hole under Dad's workbench and. . . ." She went on to tell how she'd discovered the discrepancy in the length of the garage and carriage room, the panel, the secret room, Oscar's letter, Blackie's kittens, the wobbly trunk, the trap door, the well, the door at the bottom of the well, and how she'd trapped herself, and of her long, desperate imprisonment, her finding the LABYRINTH, her searching in the corridors, the pointing box that wasn't empty, finding Oscar's string, coming to HALL, and then hitting her head just when freedom was a step away.

"Blast it!" burst from Oscar when she stopped

for breath. "Why wasn't it me? The best part of the Secret and me dillydallying with my stupid cousins in Shaker Heights."

"Thank God you weren't down there with her," Dad said. "If it hadn't been for you, Oscar, we wouldn't have known about the false wall. . . ."

"And I'd still be down there if it hadn't been for Big Oscar and Pete." Kate shuddered.

"Oh no you wouldn't!" Dad exclaimed. "We were hot on your trail because of Little Oscar here."

"Yeah, Oscar's the one who. . . ." Simone butt in, but Oscar said,

"Let me tell." And for once Simone yielded gracefully.

"I don't know exactly when the letter came because we were in Shaker Heights visiting these relatives, see; but when we got home I grabbed it and went to my room to decipher it when Simone came bursting in saying you'd been kidnapped. I didn't believe it, but she got the paper, and there was your picture staring out at me, big as life. So then I deciphered the letter real quick, and I told Mom about our searching for the Secret and all, and she got Flint, and we all came down here right away."

"I was so worried." Mrs. Witherspoon frowned behind her manicured fingers.

"You were a sight for sore eyes," Dad said. "I was

about plum crazy by then. When we read the letter, we all rushed out to the carriage room, and that's when you showed up, you and Big Oscar and Pete. So, we were hot on your trail, Kate, and we would have found you in a little while. . . ."

"She really got herself out," Nathan said quietly. Those five words made Kate very happy.

"Let's go exploring the LABYRINTH." Josh leaped up.

"No," Dad said. "That'll have to wait for later. It's really something." He scratched his head. "All that cave right here under our land all these years, and it takes you two kids to find it. Caves like the ones in the lake bluffs; and then all these mottos, wells and codes . . . the whole Underground Railroad. It beats any story I ever read."

"Even Sherlock Holmes," Oscar said.

"Who's he?" Josh asked.

"Enough." Mrs. Witherspoon stood up on her wonderfully high heels. "Kate isn't completely over this terrible ordeal, and she must rest. Children, get into your bathing suits and we'll spend the afternoon at the lake. And, Edgar, don't forget, dinner with us at the mansion at half-past seven this evening."

"I won't forget," Dad said.

Flint held his face rigid as the children swarmed into the limousine in their bathing suits and plopped down on the spotless beige upholstery. They drove off, waving and hooting.

Kate and Dad watched them. And then Mr. Elmer brought a glass of water and a tiny green pill, and the next thing Kate knew it was evening.

# Chapter 19

Everyone had to take a bath as if it were Saturday and church was the next day, instead of Monday and just a visit next door. They all put on their Sunday clothes, and Dad lined them up for inspection as they waited for the limousine. Josh and Nathan got to sit in front with Flint and watch all the glowing dials on the wood-paneled dashboard. Mr. Elmer refused to go. No place to spit.

When they entered the great tiled foyer of the mansion, Old Mr. Porch and Mrs. Witherspoon greeted them. Mrs. Witherspoon looked like a queen in shimmering chiffon that swept the floor. It smelled like lilacs when she moved.

"Welcome, neighbor." Old Mr. Porch leaned on his cane and held out his hand to Dad to whom he'd never before spoken in Kate's memory. She stood watching the adults, weak and ill at ease. Her patent leather shoes pinched. Then Oscar came swinging into the hall on his crutches. "Come along, Kate. Big Oscar and Pete are in the library." His bow tie was red polka dots.

"Sissy," Josh hissed as Oscar went by, but Simone heard and punched him. Everyone followed them into the book-lined room. Big Oscar and Pete stood there, shifting uncomfortably in new suits.

"Hi, Kate," they said. She smiled shyly, really glad to see them. Oscar drew her across the thick carpet to the desk. There lay the box. Everyone gathered round.

"It's just like the others, Kate. . . ." Oscar began.

"What others?" Josh asked.

"Other boxes," Oscar explained. "This is the fourth box we've found, all exactly alike."

"But where did you find them?" Josh had to know everything all at once.

"Guess I didn't tell you that part," Oscar said. "In HALL, that's where."

"Josh, you remember that day I broke my arm, don't you?" Kate asked. "You dared me to spy on the hobo camp with you and. . . ." She turned to the others. "Well, that day Josh and I saw a fight. Two hobos beat up on another one and stole his chicken. They ran away, but they hid on the path, and Josh and I ran into them coming back to the steps, so we went running up the bank, and I fell and broke my arm and found HALL. That's Oscar's and my code word for cave. And then Oscar and Simone came, and I told them about the Strawbridge Secret, and then Oscar broke his ankle and we formed Cripples Incorporated. We began reading books about the Underground Railroad, and one said that HALLS . . . caves . . . were used as hiding places, so I told Oscar about my cave and. . . ."

"Why didn't you tell me?" Simone demanded, mad as a wet bee that she hadn't been included.

"You didn't want to play with us cripples."

"And we decided to explore HALL," Oscar said. "We got matches and candles and strings and flashlights and food and water and a knife and . . ."

"My Scout knife?" Nathan asked. Kate nodded.

"And we found this passageway that looked like a mine shaft and had wooden supports and all, then we found these panels and the door through them, and that passage went around the HALL-in and then we came to the real natural HALL. And that's where the first box was," Oscar said.

"But we couldn't get it open. We had to loosen the latch with the hatchet, but it was empty," Kate said.

"Then we began exploring with our strings and found lots of passageways and corridors and empty boxes. . . ."

"Oscar," Kate interrupted. "Know what those boxes were there for?"

"No, what?"

"They were markers. Remember the first one we found in HALL? I'm almost positive they were markers. That first one pointed to the passageway that led to the tunnel that connected our HALL to the slave HALL, but we were too dumb to know that."

"I said not to pick that box up when we found it, remember?" Oscar couldn't help boasting.

"I remember all right, but we did pick it up anyway."

"And the other boxes we found were always where the corridors divided."

"Yeah, you're right."

"What was in the boxes?" Nathan asked slowly.

"Nothing . . . just locked empty boxes. That's what didn't make sense."

"Did you explore all the LABYRINTH?" Josh asked impatiently.

"No," Kate said. "Mom found out about HALL because I asked her about those loony Strawbridge twins. And she forbade us going exploring any more. So then we went to the guest room where the twins had died, and we searched and didn't find anything except the motto, but Mrs. Witherspoon came home from New York just then, so we had to communicate in code and write letters to each other."

"What was the code?" Simone jumped forward.

"Easy," Oscar grinned. "Just the alphabet backwards. *A* was 26 and *B* was 25 and *C* was 24 . . ."

Oscar looked smugly at Kate. "Kate would be 1626722."

"Oh." Simone sounded like a deflated balloon.

"I found this box where the tunnel divided three different ways. It was pointing down the left corridor, and I went that way, and that's how I came to the string that Oscar and I had used to explore the LABYRINTH. But you know all that. So this box is just like all those others," she finished. Her hand went out and touched the box. "You've opened it," she said sadly.

"No, Kate, I just got the lock off, but I've been saving it for you to open. It's *your* box." They laughed at their private joke.

"Come on, Kate, quit stalling," Josh said.

A hush fell over the room. Slowly she lifted the lid, leaned forward, and looked inside. Simone and Josh poked their heads closer and stared in.

A bundle of red cloth lay in the corner. She took it in trembling hands, and began to unwind the faded velvet. As the last wrappings came off, out fell a small leather book. Kate picked it up. On the front were the faint gilt letters:

DIARY

She held it out for all to see.

"Open it, Kate," Dad said solemnly. She did. It was

old and rather crumbly so she handled it reverently. On the flyleaf in slanted purple ink was written:

*Victory Ann Strawbridge*
*My Diary*

She turned the page.

I, Victory Ann Strawbridge, being in excellent health and of sound mind . . .

"Sound mind?" Oscar drew back. "She was loony as all get out." He obviously was thinking of the boxes as markers then. "Or maybe not, maybe . . ."

"Don't interrupt," Simone ordered.

. . . sound mind do take my pen in hand to record for posterity the secrets that were wrought in this, the Strawbridge Place, in Ashtabula, Ohio, in this year of our Lord, 185 . . .

Kate stopped, squinting down at the page. "The writing fades in and out," she said to the ring of faces around her.

"She's one of the ones who made up the motto, isn't she?" Simone demanded.

"I think so."

"I still don't understand about that," Simone said.

"But that's the easiest part," Oscar said. And he went on to repeat:

## THE LIBERTY WELL

MEASURE FOR MEASURE
ROUND STEPS, THEN THE LABYRINTH
TRUTH AND FREEDOM
HIDDEN FROM FALSE MEN
EMPTY IT SEEMS
BUT THEREIN LIES THE TALE

"You see . . ." He and Kate began talking in turns.

"The LIBERTY WELL is the cistern. . . ."

". . . And MEASURE FOR MEASURE is twenty-one and fifteen," said Kate.

"ROUND STEPS . . . the iron ones in the well . . . THEN THE LABYRINTH . . . the slave cave. . . ." Oscar said.

"TRUTH AND FREEDOM/HIDDEN FROM FALSE MEN . . . so the whole family acted crazy to protect the slaves."

"EMPTY IT SEEMS/BUT THERIN LIES THE TALE . . . empty boxes pointing the way through the LABYRINTH . . . all empty but this one, and therein is the tale . . . Victory's diary."

"And this should explain all." Oscar's eyes glowed.

"But it's so faded, Oscar." Kate leaned over the little book. "It'll take us a long time to figure it out."

"So what? Think what fun it'll be, and we have the whole rest of the summer. Cripples Incorporated, onward and upward." Oscar saluted her.

"Dinner is served," announced Maida in a surly voice from the doorway. Old Mr. Porch approached Margaret, bowed, and held out his arm.

"May I have the pleasure of escorting you in to dinner, Mistress Cummings?" His eyes twinkled. Hesitantly Margaret put her hand through his arm, and they went toward the dining room, Old Mr. Porch listing to Margaret's side like a schooner before the wind.

Dad extended his arm to Mrs. Witherspoon, and she took it joyfully. Kate took Oscar's arm. Josh minced to Simone and held out his arm, and she simpered as she took it, but she tripped Josh as they entered the dining room. Pete and Big Oscar and Nathan came last. They all sat down. Old Mr. Porch said the blessing. Maida began circling the table with various dishes. Kate didn't serve herself and sat staring at Mrs. Witherspoon.

"Eat, dear." Mrs. Witherspoon looked down at Kate's empty plate.

"Mrs. Witherspoon, may I ask you something?"

"Why, of course, dear." Mrs. Witherspoon leaned

toward her, smiling and listening.

"Why does Mom call you Elizabeth?"

"You mean I'm another mystery to you?" she said. "It's very simple, really. Your mother and I were in college together years ago in New York. She was a freshman when I was a senior, but I met Oscar and Simone's daddy there in my senior year, dropped out and got married. So we didn't have much time to get acquainted, but we did know each other a little bit. After all, we were the only two girls in the whole college from Ashtabula. But I really didn't know your mother. I never met her here because I went to boarding school in the east and never had any Ashtabula friends, not even your sweet mother even though she lived here in the Strawbridge Place just down the hill."

"Oh," Kate sighed. Maida humped back in with all the dishes, and Kate filled her plate. But then she sat and stared at it, and soon the tears were running down her face.

"Now what's the matter?" Josh asked in a disgusted voice.

"Mom," Kate cried. "She isn't here." Mrs. Witherspoon laughed happily.

"Why, Kate, just think how lucky you are? When she gets home, you can tell her all your adventures over again."

"Three times." Margaret counted on her fat fingers. "One time to Mommy and two times to the twins."

Dad smiled so broadly that Kate did too. She began to eat.

# CODE TRANSLATIONS

*Text of coded letter on page 117.*

ARE YOU WORKING ON MOTTO? I AM READING
S. HOLMES. HE IS HARD. CAN YOU SNEAK AWAY? HOT,
HUH? MOM IS MUM ABOUT HALL SO FAR.

M'LADY

*Text of coded letter on page 118.*

READ TWO S. H. STORIES. WISH HE COULD HELP US.
HE'D MAKE MOM LET US EXPLORE HALL. HOT, HOT,
HOT. WHAT ARE YOU DOING? I'M WORKING ON MOTTO
AND GETTING NOWHERE. WRITE.

M'LADY

*Text of coded letter on page 123.*

I'M OK. HOW ARE YOU? I'M READING LOTS ABOUT
THE UNDERGROUND RAILROAD AND FEEL HALL AND
MOTTO ARE MOST IMPORTANT CLUES SO FAR. AM
READING SHERLOCK HOLMES. HAVE YOU EXPLORED
ANYMORE?

M'LORD

*Text of coded letter on page 139.*

FOUND FALSE WALL NEXT TO GARAGE À LA SHERLOCK
HOLMES IN NORWOOD BUILDER. GARAGE (21) CARRIAGE
ROOM (15). THINK BLACKIE HAD KITTENS THERE.
EXPLORING RIGHT NOW. SOME THUNDERSTORM, HUH?

M'LADY

# Helen Pierce Jacob

HELEN PIERCE JACOB was born and reared in the northeastern corner of Ohio and lived much of her life in a century-old house exactly like the Strawbridge Place. She and her sister and two brothers spent many hours searching for the Secret just as Kate and Oscar do. She also explored the riverbank, climbed trees, jumped in the haymow, sneaked across the forbidden trestle, attended church, went to Lake Erie for picnics and swimming, read, kept journals and had a horse.

Mrs. Jacob went to school and college in Ohio and has been a school and college librarian much of her life. She and her husband presently live just outside Washington, D.C.